NOW I'M PHOTOGENIC
And Other Stories I Tell Myself

JILL ROSENBERG

Black Lawrence Press

Black Lawrence Press

Executive Editor: Diane Goettel
Book Cover Design: Zoe Norvell
Cover Art: "Drifting" by Hanna Ilczyszyn
Book Interior Design: Serena Solin

ISBN: 9781625572172

Published 2026 by Black Lawrence Press.
Printed in the United States.

Contents

for my mother

The Logic of Imaginary Friends

Four hours after Cecile left for sleep-away camp, I ran into my old imaginary friend, Kopel Cooperstein.

We reunited with each other in a supermarket parking lot—actually, in my car in the parking lot. There was a little girl standing in a shopping cart not ten feet from my car, a blonde girl in a pink bikini. She was singing to her mother opera-style, arms outstretched, chin to the sun.

She looks just like Cecile did at that age, I said to myself. Then I realized I was actually talking to Kopel. Something about that girl must have made me think of him, and then there he was, sitting in the passenger seat of my car.

Kopel looked nothing like he used to, but I recognized him right away. His hair had darkened almost to black, and it was wilder than it had been. He wore thick, black plastic- framed glasses, and his eyes had turned from the dull brown they were when we were kids into an almost otherworldly green. He was wearing a polo shirt striped with different shades of lime—it matched his eyes.

I hadn't seen Kopel Cooperstein in seventeen years, not since my first day of college. It was so good to see him I felt like crying.

It was Cecile's idea to go away to camp, I told Kopel as we walked toward the market. She's eleven, I told him. She was afraid she couldn't handle it, so she had to try is what she said. She's like that.

Kopel smiled as if it made perfect sense to him that my daughter would be like this. He held my hand as we walked.

☙

The truth is, my relationship with Kopel did not end on good terms. My parents drove me to college in a small van they rented for the occasion. I sat in the very back with all of my stuff between me and them, Kopel straddling my lap, what with all my belongings leaving no other space for him.

I told him it was pathetic, what I was doing with him. That's what we talked about for most of the four-hour ride. I told him it was bad enough that he was, let's face it, my best friend, and bad enough—narcissistic and arrogant, even—to love so deeply my own invention because it was really just loving myself, wasn't it? But far worse than friendship, I knew, was letting him provide me with any further physical comfort. Because of course part of me wanted that. Part of me felt the weight of his body on my lap like he was really there, and of course I wanted him to hold me, to comfort me in any way he could because it was a big deal, my going away all alone for the first time. But the more I told myself to resist, the more I engaged with him, arguing that Kopel and I shouldn't even be talking, let alone this, whatever we were doing.

And Kopel said, What this are you referring to? What this is there really? Ask anyone and they're going to say there's nothing to see, nothing happening here at all. So if you mean this, he said, and very slowly he pressed his chest and his hips into mine. Just let me, he said. I need to, he said, and he put his hands on my neck and his fingers in my hair. Just do it, Kopel said, referring my thought, my desire, really, to give in, to wrap my arms around my body and let it—in my mind—be Kopel embracing me like that, and yet I was pushing him away all the while, not letting myself feel him on my lap. But then this drowsy feeling came over me, like I had given up, except that it felt like conquest, not like defeat, and I felt dizzy in a good way. That's when he took hold of my arms and wrapped them around me, and then he was back on my lap again and it was his arms around me.

Then there was no stopping us. Every part of him moved exactly as I wanted in every moment, the perfect pressure, just the right speed, so that I had to lean back and give in. His parts were mine to wield exactly as I liked. If I let him, he could satisfy me perfectly, I knew, for the rest of my life.

In the end it seemed like fate and even like luck or good fortune that my roommate arrived with her boyfriend that night, her real live boyfriend, who was much older than we were, who had long wavy hair like a rock star. She introduced us, and I immediately excused myself to go to the restroom. Marcy and her boyfriend smiled at me as I got up to leave, and then they started to laugh before the door had a chance to shut completely behind me.

I didn't have a choice—I had to get rid of Kopel—my future depended on it. I thought I was doing it for my own good, for the sake of my reputation and any chance I had to be happy.

I pulled Kopel into a bathroom stall with me and ended things right then and there. I ended our seven-year relationship by saying goodbye in that cramped stall and then throwing him from the fifth-floor bathroom window. I saw his body fall to the ground the way a sheet of paper might fall on a windy day. He looked up at me one last time before dashing off to the forest on the outskirts of campus. I pictured him crying and sleeping with wild animals, doves or wolves and maybe a young doe. As I said goodbye and opened the window and pushed him out, I imagined Marcy jerking off her boyfriend in my bed. I blamed her for our breakup.

After that, whenever I'd catch myself beginning to say something to Kopel out of habit, I'd try to imagine myself saying it to someone else instead, some real person actually in my life, if not within earshot. That night I had an imaginary conversation with Marcy in which I described my relationship with Kopel and our breakup earlier that day. I told her everything except for the fact that he didn't exist, and I didn't tell her that we'd broken up because of her—in a way all of that was irrelevant to my point, which was to explain that if I seemed somewhat solemn or anti-social, it was only because the breakup was so recent. In our imaginary conversation, Marcy found this story inspirational. Later that night I pictured her breaking up with her own boyfriend, in the same bathroom stall, while I brushed my teeth at the sink not ten feet away.

At that time in my life, Kopel was tall and skinny with shaggy blond hair and sulky brown eyes, which was pretty much my type back then. His new look is more suited to my current taste—I mean, of course it is. He looks like a successful lawyer who works pro-bono on weekends. Or he looks like a neurosurgeon who is also a Special Olympics coach. In other words, he looks smart and professional, impressive and even intimidating, but also sensitive, possibly understanding, if you had a story worthy of his sympathy.

As soon as we enter the supermarket and we're surround by all of these average men and women, I realize how tall he's grown. He's at least a head taller than anyone else in the store. It makes me want to wrap my arms around his shoulders and hang from him. I'd like him to carry me piggyback through the aisles. Instead, we stand and stare at the cold cereal.

I plan to eat nothing but cereal for the six weeks she's away, I tell him. No one is in the aisle with us, so I say it aloud, but quietly.

Kopel keeps his gaze on the cereal and so do I, but I picture him smiling.

I like you with this extra flesh, he says, and he shuffles himself closer to me, to show that he means it. I can feel his arm against my shoulder. It's nice, what he said. It makes me feel pretty in this way I don't usually feel pretty. But I have planned to be as waif-like as Cecile by the time she gets home from camp. I want it to be obvious to everyone that she's mine, but she has her father's build, long-limbed and lanky.

It seems strange that Kopel knows nothing about Cecile. He's not familiar with the story I've told my friends and family, that her lanky father left us when Cecile was three months old. He doesn't know that in fact I pushed her father to leave because—this is the story I tell myself—I couldn't handle loving both of them at once, and his love for Cecile seemed to threaten in some way the love I felt for both of them individually.

I start thinking that I want to tell him the whole story. I want to recount everything that's happened to me since we last saw each other. He is meanwhile filling my cart with cereal, and that's when I realize he's planning to stay with me for the duration of the six weeks. We're going to eat this cereal together, and it's such a relief I would embrace him that instant if we weren't in the supermarket and if Kopel actually existed outside my mind. His hands, I notice, have grown huge and beautiful over the years.

Is it wrong of me to stand in line at the register feeling excited about spending six weeks alone with Kopel, eating box after box of cereal and touching each other in every way I can possibly think of? Maybe for once my mind is working to help me through this, this time I have without Cecile. Maybe I shouldn't think about it too much or I'll mess it all up.

It's more than excitement; it's optimism. That's what it feels like—optimism, or maybe it's closer to pride—this feeling like I'm proud of my well-timed, almost entrepreneurial reunion with Kopel. And I'm proud of myself for feeling proud because it wasn't always this way. When I banished Kopel from my life, for example, that evening in the bathroom stall, I did so with complete blindness to the fact that our relationship made me more self-sufficient. But now I can't think of one reason why I shouldn't spend the next six weeks with him. In fact, it seems like close to the best idea I've ever had and a real mark of my maturity.

ಌ

There was a real Kopel Cooperstein, I remind Kopel on our way home. I used to listen to his Sunday night radio show, an hour-long program airing at midnight that I discovered when I was eleven.

Have I told you about the real Kopel Cooperstein? I ask Kopel, but of course I have. The real Kopel Cooperstein, I say, had a voice so deep its vibrations tickled my throat and made my skin hot in these very particular places. I'm trying to make him jealous, so I name the areas of my body I'm referring to: the hollow at the center of my back, my temples, under my arms, behind my kneecaps and along my inner thighs. The real Kopel Cooperstein, I say, could make me blush from my forehead halfway down my torso, just by introducing his guest for the evening.

Meanwhile, the imaginary Kopel and I drive home from the market, over the bridge, crossing the river that runs through town. We pass the parking lot where Cecile and I met the camp bus earlier that morning. We had to be there at 7:45, and the bus pulled away as promised by 8:01. It was a sunny morning and hard to see into the windows of the bus because of all the glare. There was one mother who practically jumped like a dog at the side of the bus, trying to get a final glimpse of her kid. My car was parked next to hers in the lot—the only two vehicles left by the time we both pulled out—and I sat in my car and watched her wail for a good fifteen minutes before driving away, her head in her hands, her back heaving. Even as she drove off, I swear I could see her shoulders trembling from the force of her crying.

By the time Kopel and I pass by the shopping center, the lot is full. People coming and going, running in here and there—it's just another normal day for most people, as most days are. For a moment I feel the emptiness of it all, and this sensation of days passing—before I know it I'll be driving up to the camp for visiting day, and then, a few weeks later, I'll return to this parking lot and it will be the bus turning the children over to their parents; it will be the parents driving away and leaving the bus behind.

I would listen to the Kopel Cooperstein Show every Sunday night in an otherwise silent house, my parents asleep down the hall. It didn't matter that I'd heard of very few of the people he interviewed. What mattered was the seriousness with which Kopel addressed his guests, the tone of his voice as he spoke about their lives as if their lives were worth speaking about.

After a while I started to make his show interactive—I'd listen to

Kopel's question and then lower the volume and answer the question myself, as if it were intended for me, the real Stella McBride.

In my mind we sat opposite one another in huge, upholstered armchairs that smelled like Kopel—the fragrance of Irish Spring soap combined with the scent of pumpkin pie—fresh and clean but also comforting. During those interviews, I was an older version of myself, one who often spoke of my experience of the world as an eleven-year-old.

The first time I thought to participate, Kopel had just asked a Cambodian performance artist if she was a very dramatic child, and she confessed that she was actually very shy. Although she didn't sound the least bit shy, I knew she was telling the truth. My heart sped up. I felt almost blanketed by this feeling of possibility that came over me in that moment. For the very first time, I realized that I could be anything I wanted to be. It was as if something warm and heavy had been draped around me, but instead of weighing me down, it infused my every movement with purpose.

I closed my eyes, and I pictured Kopel across from me. Everything came into focus. His armchair was dark gray and covered in green paisley. Mine was navy, striped with thin orange lines. Kopel wore jeans, cuffed at the ankle, black socks and big black wingtips, exactly the pair I wanted for myself. I always liked the idea of steel at my toes, and I told him so. He wore a light green button-down shirt with a tie, a look I liked a lot at the time.

I said, I was very shy, and I said it aloud. When I raised the radio's volume, I heard Kopel chuckling. That's hard to believe, he said to his Cambodian guest, but it really sounded like he was talking to me. I felt this conviction that the real Kopel Cooperstein was deeply interested in hearing anything I might say to him.

I told him I used to wake myself up in the middle of the night to listen to his show. I'd pretend that I was the one you were interviewing, I'd say, feeling bold even as I pictured him starting to blush. I'd talk to you just like I'm talking to you right now, I said. I told him it made me feel powerful and free, like I could be anyone I wanted to be. I'd picture him looking at me like I'd said something astonishing, something brilliant. I'd make eye contact with him and hold it.

I didn't tell him that after a while I didn't need him to host—I'd invent most of his questions anyway. Eventually, I didn't need the real Kopel Cooperstein at all. I didn't need the radio or the middle of the night—that feeling of freedom was mine for the taking anytime I wanted it, and so was my very own Kopel Cooperstein.

CR

Kopel and I are walking from the car to the back door of my house when I see my neighbor, Loraine, crouched down behind a bush, doing some kind of gardening work. I don't notice her until I'm already halfway up my walk, and I realize I've been whispering with Kopel, loud enough for her to hear. When I finally catch sight of her, I'm in the middle of explaining to Kopel that I moved into the house the very day Cecile was born.

I look at Loraine and Loraine stops what she's doing and looks back at me. But she doesn't look appalled or concerned, so I figure either she hasn't heard me or she thinks it's OK if I'm talking to myself. How would she know if in my head there's this image of Kopel, that in my head I'm not really talking to myself at all and that's the point.

"Have a good afternoon," she says, and she keeps her eyes on her shovel in the dirt.

"You too," I say, and I smile as if she's looking at me.

As I'm unlocking the door, I go back to whispering to Kopel, more quietly, though. I say, We're going to go inside, and we're going to put down these groceries—we don't have to put away the cereal, though I guess we should put the milk in the fridge—then I'll give you a tour of the house.

I like to tell you what we're going to do before we actually do it, I tell him. Have I always liked to do that? I do the same thing with Cecile. Even before she could talk I did it. She's been pointing it out recently. Ever since she made this decision to go away for the summer she's been noticing things about me. It's like she thinks

I'm fascinating all of sudden, though not necessarily in a good way. But I don't think it's so strange, liking to announce what's going to happen as I prepare to do it. It helps me feel more organized and intentional about what I'm doing, and I think it makes sense, I say.

We're still at the door. For some reason, I don't want to open it. I feel like I'm going to find something horrifying inside the house, police officers huddled around a murder scene or just a huge mess I don't remember making. I'll find someone else's mess, or someone else's life, maybe. I'll discover that the last eleven years have only occurred in my mind—I don't have a daughter and this isn't my home. Now that Cecile is gone, it seems impossible that we ever lived together in this house.

We might not live here, I say to Kopel. I don't think this is my house.

Let's go in anyway, Kopel says. And right in front of me, he grows another inch taller. He's got to be six-five, a whole foot taller than me. He could carry me on his back for miles if I wanted him to. He looks at me and I watch his eyes get even greener. I've always wanted eyes like that, and so I give them to Kopel.

He looks amazing, but I still feel a little bit nervous, a little bit lonely, and then, out of nowhere, Kopel's wearing my father's red Christmas sweater. It has to be ninety degrees out, and I do feel kind of bad, putting him in this ridiculous sweater, but I love the idea of him wearing it. He likes it too—I can tell. The sweater seems to fill him with the spirit of Christmas. His smile is huge. We both feel happier. When I put my hand on the doorknob, he starts to smell like cinnamon.

The back door opens to the kitchen, and we walk in to find the huge mess Cecile and I really did leave behind us. Our dirty breakfast dishes are still on the table, two tiny, jagged bite marks missing from Cecile's toast. Her red hooded sweatshirt hangs from the back of her chair, and her slippers wait under the table, as if she's just in the other room and she'll come back for them when she gets cold.

We both prefer to keep the house cold because we like to bundle up, but now it feels too cold, like something's wrong. It's so quiet I almost forget that Kopel is in the room with me—then the refrigerator starts to hum, and it actually startles me, sends a tingling sensation from my elbows to my fingertips. Kopel wraps his arms around me from behind, and I let myself lean into him.

This is the kitchen, I say, starting the tour. Hunter—that's Cecile's father—he's the one who hung the wallpaper. And I realize right then that I almost never think about this, but he told me that no one would notice if there was no wallpaper behind the refrigerator. He said no one would look back there.

Kopel is sitting at the two-person kitchen table, his hands behind his head as listens to me. And he looks exactly like Hunter. He has Hunter's blond hair, his dark blue eyes, and this expression on his face like he's blissfully happy but probably a little bit dim. He crosses his legs the way Hunter did, one foot tucked behind the calf of his other leg, like two willowy strands of a braid. He's not wearing the Christmas sweater anymore.

I stand in my kitchen, staring at Kopel looking exactly like Hunter, and it occurs to me that I could kiss him. I start walking toward him. He still has his hands up on his head, and he's smiling like he's daring me to do it. I'm feeling good again—that free feeling, like I can do anything I want.

I stand close enough that he could touch me. Did I tell you I'm a journalist? I'm a journalist, I tell Kopel/Hunter. And for a minute I'm confused about which Kopel this is—the real Kopel Cooperstein or the imaginary one—and I almost tell him that he was my inspiration. Did you know that your old shows were podcasted? I ask him, and I grab his hands from his head and I put them on my hips; then I'm hugging him and I'm crying. I sit on his lap and I push myself into him.

I love you, I say. I say it like I'm the romantic lead in a movie, like I'm lanky and gorgeous. Then I press my lips into his and press the back of his head to the wall. I let myself enjoy it, kissing all three of them at once—Hunter, the real Kopel Cooperstein, and the one I made up. And it doesn't feel pathetic, not at all. No one knows what I'm doing anyway—if I don't think it's pathetic, then it's not.

CR

That evening, Kopel and I sit on my porch eating Frosted Flakes and drinking alcoholic lemonade. Earlier in the week Cecile hung Christmas lights and a string of red lanterns around the porch. It's not quite dark yet, but I turn them on anyway.

The porch is nicely positioned at the side of the house—I have a view of the street, but I can also see into the yards of my neighbors. I can see Loraine's well-groomed yard to the left, and I can see onto the front lawns across the street. In the backyard behind mine, two teenagers are trying to make use of a kiddy pool they have on their lawn. They squirt each other with the hose, the girl standing in the turquoise plastic pool. I watch her lift her bikini top, letting the boy—who is either her brother or looks exactly like her brother—aim the stream of water at her bare breasts.

Kopel lies back on a lounge chair. There's an empty chair between us, where Cecile has abandoned another sweatshirt. Kopel stretches out on the lounge chair. He's wearing my father's Christmas sweater again, with a pair of green swim trunks. He is also rubbing my feet.

Cecile's sweatshirt looks almost like a small animal, a skinny old alley cat that used the last of its strength to crawl up onto that chair, curl itself into a ball and die. I've always wanted a cat, I tell Kopel, but Cecile is allergic to them. And that's when it occurs to me—I hold Cecile's sweatshirt in a bundle on my lap, and then there's my cat. His name is Kopel, I tell Kopel. Pet him, I say, and Kopel pets the cat.

I'm a little bit drunk, busy petting my kitten and being interviewed by Kopel when my six-year-old neighbor, Mika, comes into my yard and then up onto the porch.

Hi, Mrs. McBride, he says. He doesn't smile. Is Cecile here? he asks me, and then he does smile. I have never felt any particular affection for Mika, but I find myself wanting to hold him in my lap.

Have a seat, Mika, I say. How are you? I ask him.

He walks over to the chair next to mine. He stands in front of it but doesn't sit down.

Do you like cats? I ask Mika.

Yes, he tells me, but I'm allergic. He holds his palms up in the air. What can you do? his palms seem to be saying. He looks up at the Christmas lights and Chinese lanterns. He shifts his weight from one leg to the other, like he's dancing for me.

Is Cecile here? he asks again. His eyes dart around my porch, as if he's suspicious and searching for evidence. But then he sits down.

I finish my fourth lemonade, tip the bottle to the sky and drain it. Cecile's not here, I tell him.

Mika nods. Oh, he says. He keeps nodding, and then I nod too. When I look over at Kopel, he's nodding along with us and smiling like he thinks I'm funny. Mika smiles too, and then he's staring at the ceiling again.

Why did you hang your Christmas lights already? he asks me.

I like Christmas, I explain. Don't you?

But it's the summer, he says. He bends forward from the waist and starts to scratch his ankle. He has very pale skin. Freckles cover most of his body. His legs have some dark hair on them already, which seems incredibly sad to me.

Do you have any imaginary friends? I ask him. I smile. You can tell me, I say.

He sits up and looks straight at me. Not really, he says.

I have an imaginary friend, I tell him.

Mika stares out into the yard; then he looks toward his own house. I start to imagine myself pulling him onto my lap, but I stop myself.

I have an imaginary friend, I repeat. He's sitting next to you, actually. Other way, I tell him. There, I say, and I point to the recliner.

Mika nods and bounces in his seat. If you're allergic to cats, I say to him, why don't you get yourself an imaginary cat? You wouldn't be allergic to an imaginary cat, would you?

He giggles, but it seems forced. No, he says, serious again. Is Cecile at sleep-away camp? he asks me. His eyes widen, and they seem to grow bigger as I look into them. All of a sudden he looks so sad and sweet that he's adorable. His too tiny nose and mouth are precious, I realize, and his big cheeks look so soft I'm tempted to reach for them.

Six weeks, I tell him.

Kopel the human and Kopel the kitten both look up at me. Then human Kopel stands up and takes off my dad's Christmas sweater. He's bare-chested. He takes the kitten from my lap and knocks the sweatshirt to the ground in the process.

You should consider getting an imaginary cat, I tell Mika. Do you want me to help you pick one? We could go to the imaginary pound right now! They're open all night, I say. The way it comes out, it sounds like I'm talking about a strip club.

I don't think about the fact that Mika is imaginary too until he turns into the four-year-old girl I saw earlier in the day, the opera singer. She agrees to go to the pound with me. She really loves the idea.

ᘓ

We end up crouched down under a small tree in my backyard—me, all three Kopels, Mika, the imaginary Hunter, and the four-year-old in the pink bikini. An imaginary version of the topless teenaged girl has come along too.

We need lots of kittens, I say to the imaginary guy working at the imaginary pound. We'd like a litter's worth, I say, and everyone else nods and smiles.

But the man shakes his head. All the kittens are at camp, he tells me.

I hear Mika's fast intake of breath in disappointment, and his chubby hand squeezes my forearm. I see the real Kopel Cooperstein reaching out, and I think he's going to touch the teenager's breasts, but instead he holds each of mine in one of his hands. The teenager puts her hands over his. My Kopel hugs me from behind and puts his hands on top of hers. Hunter gives the girl from the shopping cart a boost, and she climbs to the top of the tree. We all watch Kopel the kitten run away, out into the street. The girl begins singing, but her voice isn't human—she's singing like a dove, coo-cooing.

I picture Cecile up at the top of the tree with her. She holds the girl's hand. She opens her mouth to sing along, but no sound comes out. Then everyone but my Kopel disappears.

I really think she's scared, I tell him. I don't think she was ready for this.

When he tries to comfort me, tries to hug and kiss me, I push him away.

I can't choose you over her, I explain.

Then I take him inside and give him the rest of the house tour because I realized I never finished it. When we're done, I put him to bed in Cecile's room. I give him a kiss on the forehead and a quick hug. I tuck him in tight and I tell him a bedtime story, a true story about my former college roommate, Marcy.

Before she could let herself have any sex fantasy, I tell him, she had to imagine her boyfriend dying and she had to mourn his death. She had to imagine it in detail and really feel the sadness of it. Only then could she allow herself to enjoy her fantasy.

CR

At one o'clock that morning, the phone rings. I'm certain it's the camp, calling to tell me that Cecile can't handle it, that she's miserable and it's too much for her bunkmates to take. They're afraid her homesickness will spread like a virus through the camp. I start to feel frantic, like I can't get to her soon enough. I feel every emotion she must be feeling, and I know she won't feel any better until I'm actually there, until she's in my arms and I'm driving us home. It's the only thing that calms me—this thought of us in the car, her warm head in my lap as I drive. I picture her falling asleep, exhausted from all that she put herself through. I picture all of this in the few seconds it takes me to walk ten feet to answer the phone.

I'm not even sure if I've said hello when I hear this almost cackling wail, and for a second I think it's someone I don't know—that's how foreign and strange it sounds—someone who's in the process of being murdered and they've called me by accident, trying to reach 911 or a neighbor. Then I hear a girl's voice in the background. She says, "Cecile, hurry!" and she sounds like she's crying too. I want to talk but I can't get myself to say anything. It feels like my heart has catapulted from my chest to my feet and I can't seem to breathe. I can't even form a concrete thought about what might be happening on the other end of the line—there's just this intense feeling of panic until I hear Cecile's voice. "Mom?" she says, "Mom, can you hear me?" She sounds out of breath and I can't help it, I start yelling at her—it's what I do when I'm worried. I'm begging her to tell what's happening, but she's wailing so hard she can't talk.

"You need to tell me if you're OK," I manage to say calmly, and that's when she stops crying—only, in that second, I realize she isn't crying—she's laughing, laughing hysterically.

"God, Mom, I'm fine!" she says. It starts a chorus of laughter around her. "We snuck out," she says. "Me and these girls from my bunk. I just wanted to say hi. We found this payphone."

She sounds happy. She sounds like she's having fun. But I still feel leftover panic. My toes are tingling from it.

"You're OK?" I ask, just to be sure.

"Yeah," she says, but she sounds distracted. In the background I can still hear laughter, and then the same girl as before telling her to hurry. "Mom," she says, "I've got to go."

The tingling is getting worse—it's getting almost painful and it's traveling up my calves. I feel like I've lost her. I sit down on my bed. It seems possible she's going to tell me that she wants to stay at camp year-round, that the camp runs a boarding school during the year and she wants to go. I imagine myself having to pack all of her stuff and send it there.

She's laughing again, and the sound of it seems to collect at the back of my throat in a giant lump.

"I love you," I say. It feels like it's the last thing I'll ever get to say to her.

"Uh huh," she says, and my eyes well up with tears. Then I realize she wasn't talking to me. "What, Mom?" she says. "I didn't hear you."

"I-love-you," I repeat, and my voice sounds awful, the way it used to sound when I'd talk to girls who were popular and prettier than me.

Before she says anything else, we get cut off. I sit there, stunned. I stare at the phone, willing it to ring. Then I lie on my side on the bed.

I tell myself she's gone forever, that I need to accept it, that this is what parents must do.

That's when I see Kopel. He's on the ceiling. He's been there, I realize, watching. Guess what? he says. Real kittens never go to camp.

I picture these real kittens, spotted and striped, on the bed, curled around me. Then I picture them running off, slipping through my fingers, out the window and down to the street.

So many choices, right? Kopel says. So many ways this could go.

He lowers a hand. It's wrapped in tinsel and covered in glitter. I can feel it inside me too, something sparkling. The kittens are back in my bed and then gone, back again and then gone for good.

I reach for Kopel's hand, then he's on the bed with me. Then he is the bed, holding me up, wrapped around me.

There was a real Kopel Cooperstein, he reminds me. We're everywhere, he whispers.

This is Fatherhood

Harold Stiller returned from a successful dinner meeting to find his daughter sleeping in his bed, holding onto his wife. In the dark bedroom, from a slight distance, their two bodies appeared to be one form. The way that his daughter had her body curled, it looked like an extension of his wife's belly, as if—again—his wife were pregnant with the child.

It wasn't until he reached the side of the bed that Harold could actually see what was happening: his wife's nightshirt was pushed up to her chin, and his five-year-old daughter had her mouth on his wife's left nipple. The child sucked absentmindedly, on and off as she slept. Harold could hear the familiar sound of his wife breathing in her sleep.

This is not my family, he thought to himself.

The pink sheet was darkened where the child's saliva had slid from his wife's breast onto the mattress. Harold was reminded of his daughter's infancy, when her constant nursing left sour-smelling wet spots on the bed that never seemed to dry.

Perhaps this transpired while they slept, he thought. For a moment he was almost touched, almost in awe. They were lovely really, his wife and his daughter, comforting one another in their sleep. It was wrong for Harold to stay out so late and leave them alone like this. They were both so delicate, so overwhelmingly female.

Harold decided to wake his daughter quietly, in order to avoid rousing his wife, to protect her from needless shame. He gripped the child's shoulder, pulled her slowly from his wife's breast. When his daughter opened her eyes, immediately wide awake, he considered kissing her forehead, but decided against it.

"It's time to go to your own bed," he whispered, trying to lift her in his arms despite her body's resistance.

"You're late," she said. "We're already sleeping." She wiggled her body out of his arms and back onto the mattress.

"I'm home now," Harold said. Part of him wanted to use his strength against her. It was easy to imagine: he could grab her more tightly; in truth, he could fling her small body from the bed with very little effort. He could get into bed with his wife and leave the child to fend for herself until morning.

Harold took a deep breath. "Come on, Ava," he said—he said it nicely, his voice practically singing the words.

"I'm sleeping here," she insisted, slapping her palm to the mattress, claiming his side of the bed.

Harold looked at the child's small fingers outstretched on the sheet. Her nails were painted with the same dark purple polish his wife had been wearing since he met her. "You always get to sleep with Mommy," the girl complained.

Usually Harold was energized by his own feelings of anger and frustration—at the office, they tended to work in his favor and fuel his productivity— but the more his daughter argued with him, the more exhausted and defeated he felt.

Finally, his wife opened her eyes, looked at Harold and smiled. Heidi had dark lips and pale skin everywhere else. Her nose was long and angular, but somehow there was a softness to her face, the pink swell at her cheeks and the fullness of her lips creating this delicate balance that made her beauty striking rather than harsh. *Harold's beautiful wife*. It's how everyone in his family referred to Heidi.

"This is my bed," he told his daughter. "Mine and your mother's. You have your own bed to sleep in."

Heidi said nothing. She lay still and silent on her side of the bed, her chest still exposed, her left nipple shiny with the girl's spit and slightly swollen. As if trying to block his view, Ava backed up against her mother, out of Harold's reach.

"I'm getting ready for bed now," Harold announced, and in response his daughter rocked her body against her mother's, and Heidi put her arm around the girl. "When I come back," Harold said, "she's going to her room."

"OK," Heidi said, and she kissed the back of the girl's head. "Go ahead," she said to Harold, but he stayed at the side of the bed.

When Ava was a baby, Heidi would often send Harold out of the room as she tried to lull the child to sleep. One night, when Ava was particularly agitated, Harold, out of concern, stood in the doorway to make sure they were OK. Ava wasn't walking yet, but she held onto the crib's railing and pulled herself up onto her feet, where she bounced clumsily and, with one hand, reached for her mother, almost losing her balance as she swatted at Heidi's chest, attempting to grab hold of her breast, as if it were no different than any other object in the infant's world, there for her to take and consume. Harold stood in that doorway and watched his wife reach her hand into her brassiere and pull her breast out over her shirt. Holding the child steady with her other hand, she leaned forward and fed her just like that, Ava's head flung back and Heidi's heavy breast hanging down into the child's mouth.

Heidi must have felt self-conscious all of a sudden, once it was happening, because she turned and looked to the doorway, only to find Harold still standing there, watching them. She waved her arm at him, wanting him to leave, but Harold found it difficult to move or even look away. He remembered the mobile, a constellation of blown glass spheres, that spun above Heidi's head as this was happening, thinking that it was the slow, steady speed of its rotation that was making him feel so dizzy.

It wasn't possible that the girl, at five years old, was still nursing. Harold reminded himself that he had regular, physical contact with his wife and knew this for a fact. Still, part of him worried that, if he left them alone for even a moment, they'd return to the state in which he'd found them, the girl's mouth clasped over his wife's nipple like it was something that belonged to her.

Your wife is sexy, his intern had said a few days before, leaning down to look at the picture of Heidi that Harold kept on his desk.

"Are you going or not?" Ava asked him. Sometimes the tone of her voice when she spoke to him was so devoid of respect Harold felt not annoyed or insulted but pathetic, as if he and Heidi had somehow created a monster who would soon overtake them both.

The side of the girl's head was pressed to her mother's on Harold's pillow, their long hair—Heidi's slightly darker and Ava's a little bit blonde—intermingled on the pillow and over their shoulders.

Ava stared up at Harold and widened her eyes. "Go!" she said. "Stop standing there!"

When he didn't move, she turned her head from Harold to face her mother. "It's not fair," she complained. "You two sleep together every night, and I have to sleep all alone in a tiny bed." She began to whimper.

Heidi pressed her palm to the top of the girl's head. "When you get married," she said, "you can have a big bed, and you can sleep with your husband like Daddy and I sleep together." She moved her smile from Harold to the girl and back again, as if to say, *Just look at us, Harold! Just look at what we made!*

Ever since Ava was born, Heidi had developed a cutesy, almost fairytale view of their lives. There were things that were good and things that were bad, a right way to do things and a wrong way. Harold supposed this was something almost evolutionarily predetermined, this ability to guide one's offspring in a way that a child could understand. In truth, Harold was sometimes comforted by it himself.

"Married people sleep in big beds," his wife consoled, "and little girls sleep in little beds. It's just the way it is."

Ava flung herself onto her back and crossed her arms at her chest. "I don't want to get married," she said. "I want to sleep with you!" She stretched one of her legs across her mother's hips and left it there.

Every night Harold watched his daughter's body contort this way, into utter desperation. She rarely slept through the night without rushing to their room for comfort. It was heartbreaking, really, her overwhelming need.

Heidi stroked Ava's head, and the girl began to relax. For a moment, Harold wanted to get into the bed with them, to comfort his daughter and give her what she wanted, but as usual, he felt unwelcome.

At breakfast that morning, Harold had watched his wife and daughter make faces at one another, some kind of staring contest they played on and off at almost every meal, a game that never included Harold. Ava sat with her feet on her chair, knees to her chest, and her shins pressed to the table. "What's on the agenda for this weekend?" Harold had asked, trying to engage with them.

"How come you always ask that?" Ava said in response. When Harold didn't answer her immediately, the girl tilted her head and stared at him. She dropped her legs to the floor and crossed her arms in front of her chest. She lifted her shoulders to her ears and mimicked him: *What's on the agenda for today*, she said and sighed, her voice deep and full of mock anger.

"Is that what I sound like to you?" Harold asked.

The girl looked at her mother and nodded, this huge, exaggerated nod that made her giggle. The giggle turned into a full laugh, Ava's mouth open so wide Harold could see bits of pancake in her teeth and on her tongue. She pounded her fists to the table a couple of times before Heidi put a hand on the girl's shoulder to calm her.

Now Ava was lying on her back in his bed, sucking on the middle and ring fingers of her left hand, her pinky and forefinger propped against her upper lip, her head tipped against her mother's shoulder. A dimple appeared and disappeared on the child's right cheek as she sucked. It was exactly the way Harold sucked his fingers as a baby, but unlike his daughter, Harold had stopped sucking by the time he was six months old.

Still, the first time he saw her doing it—the day she was born—Harold was so touched he stood in front of the mirror in the hospital bathroom, his fingers in his mouth that way for the first time since he was a baby. He hadn't realized until then that he also had a dimple on his right cheek. It almost seemed like proof that she might actually be his, although the chance of that, he knew, was less than point five percent. Heidi acted as if of course the child were his, and they didn't tell anyone else about what they had done. They didn't even tell their parents.

Early on, as an infant at least, Ava did look like Harold, but he knew even then that he wasn't her real father. Even before the doctor confirmed that the procedure had worked, Harold knew. He could tell that Heidi had conceived because she started to smell slightly sour to him, or rotten, the way people sometimes smell different and off-putting when they're sick, almost like a natural warning to those around them. If Ava were his child biologically, certainly he wouldn't have felt repelled by her in this way.

When Harold pictured the procedure that had created his daughter, he saw Heidi with her hips lifted in the air and a doctor between her legs, funneling thick, fetid semen into his beautiful wife. Heidi insisted on going to the fertility clinic alone. Harold knew she was trying to save him the humiliation—she didn't want him sitting at her side, obviously the deficient one. Harold's beautiful, capable wife, on her back, alone in a hospital bed in a different city, so that no one (not even Heidi's obstetrician), would know what they had done.

And Harold would wait for her at a nearby hotel—they spent way more than they could afford at the time on that hotel because neither of them could handle it if the room were even the slightest bit seedy. She'd come to the room and lie on her back on the bed, and he had to make himself come inside her. She barely moved, braced herself there on the bed, as if there were already a delicate, fully formed baby inside her and she was afraid he might hurt it. But this was part of the procedure, a way to include poor Harold and ensure that they would never be certain if the child were his or not—the doctor had actually said this—but Harold knew they were just humoring him, the way you humor a child, asking him to open a jar for you after you've already loosened the lid. Harold really had no part in creating his daughter—it was the doctor, the donor, and Heidi, as a trio, who brought the child into the world, a feat more impressive than any other he'd witnessed in his life, and Harold's only role was to pretend he'd been involved.

Heidi did everything she could to make him feel otherwise. She was adamant that they request a donor who was exactly like Harold—she weighed and measured him, took photographs and pulled hair from his head to include with their portfolio. A Jewish lawyer, she'd even insisted, although, in those days, almost all of the donors were medical students. He was lucky, he supposed, that they ended up with Ava, a sort of extension of her mother who seemed so completely girl that it was hard to imagine any part of her was made by a man.

As soon as Heidi stopped nursing, she smelled like herself again. It was such a relief to Harold that he found himself pressing his nose to the top of her head as often as he could, just to reassure himself that the change hadn't been permanent.

"I'm tired," he told his wife now. "I've had a long day. She needs to go to her room."

"OK," Heidi agreed. Her hand stroked the girl's head. "As soon as you come back. Go ahead," she said, and then she pulled her nightshirt down over her chest and smiled at Harold, as if she knew all along what was worrying him. "Go get washed up," she said.

Their bathroom looked like something you'd find in a boutique hotel—white marble walls with swirls of gray, see-through glass shower doors and a jacuzzi tub, two sinks that looked like fancy serving bowls, so that Harold always felt like he was doing something wrong when he spit into them.

There was a large window just behind the toilet through which Harold could see most of his backyard. It was the backyard that convinced him to buy the house. The kidney-shaped swimming pool was surrounded by lush and dark green foliage that, at this time of year, was just shy of overgrown.

The previous owners installed floodlights in some of the trees, and Heidi, as a surprise for Harold, had a switch for those lights installed just next to the toilet so that he could stand there and look out at his yard, even at night.

He had four flowerbeds in his view from the bathroom, petals in every color you could imagine. But what Harold loved most were the trees—he had twenty-one trees on the property, including a number of enormous sycamores and lindens, a few of which had been growing on the land for over a hundred years. The trees were so plentiful, so big, that their long, thick branches and ample leaves blocked his view of virtually everything but the sky that lay beyond his property line. Harold owned those trees just like he owned the house. He owned the beautiful grass and paid another man to mow it.

As a child, he hadn't known it was possible to own elements of nature. The trees on his street in Brooklyn belonged to the city, to all of his neighbors. He lived in a one-bedroom apartment with his parents and slept in the living room, which also served as his father's study. His father's newspapers were stacked on every surface, and even Harold's small dresser was filled mostly with his father's books. His father, who had never had the opportunity to attend college, was nonetheless setting an example for his son—*a boy must study!*—he'd say to Harold, allowing him only an hour a day to play outside with his friends. But Harold never felt deprived, and he liked sleeping in the living room. It made him feel mature and responsible, as if he had a post at the front of the apartment, and it was his job to remain at his post and protect his family as they slept.

His father still lived in that small apartment, though his mother passed away just one month after Ava was born. According to the doctors, Harold's infertility was likely caused by a complication when he was in utero, a medication his mother was given while she was pregnant with him, although Harold never told his mother anything about this. She met Ava only once, sitting in that very living room.

"I think she looks just like me," his mother had said, smiling down at this baby who belonged, really, to a stranger, a man and his family whose name they would never know, and Harold's mother sat there brimming with pride, having no idea that she'd produced a son who was basically a dud. Of course his mother couldn't have begun to guess what they'd done—chances were she had no idea it was even possible to make a baby the way they had—it would have seemed like science fiction to her, or the realm of the rich and famous. *I couldn't be happier*, she'd said that night. *I couldn't be more proud.*

Harold felt so ashamed for her in that moment he could barely stand to look at the gleeful expression on her face. "She's too emotional. It's embarrassing," he told Heidi as soon as they were out the door.

After that one time, they made excuses to avoid seeing his parents until his father called one night to say that his mother had a massive, fatal heart attack.

The truth was that the death of Harold's mother made it much easier for him to pretend that they were a regular family. In fact, he and Heidi told Ava that she took after his mother. You have the same exact body type, they'd tell her, though that was really only true when Ava was a chubby toddler. But they still went on and on about it, both of them, Harold and Heidi, saying it so often that most of the time they forgot how far from the truth it really was.

After he changed out of his clothes, brushed his teeth and washed his face and wiped down the sink, Harold rinsed the bathtub, where the child had clearly bathed that evening, though she had a bathroom of her own. There were still bubbles by the drain and one of Ava's books left on the lip of the tub. Harold wondered if Heidi had bathed with her—sometimes it was the only way to convince Ava to get clean.

In fact, he reminded himself, she'd gone through a stage when she actually liked to get into the shower with Harold. She liked to pretend that she had to get ready for work in the morning just like him. As soon as he'd start to get undressed, she'd strip down along with him and follow him into the shower. They kept a bar of soap in there for each of them—a big bar and a little heart-shaped bar, though mostly Ava would just stand with her body pressed into the corner of the stall, looking up at him, trying her best to stay out of the water.

Harold actually enjoyed their little ritual, though he was somewhat relieved when she outgrew it. It was easier to get himself showered without her right there under him, always having to worry that she was going to slip or get soap in her eyes and start screaming.

But he did wonder why things had changed, so one day he asked her about it. "How come you don't like to get ready for work with me anymore?" he said naively to the girl, who must have been three years old at the time.

"I don't like you," Ava had said in response, as if this were just a fact she'd never bothered to share.

"You don't like me?" Harold repeated, just to make sure he'd heard her correctly.

"It's your penis, Daddy," she'd explained. "I don't like your penis."

Now, he opened the bathroom window and stood in front of it bare-chested, so he could feel the warm breeze on his skin as he stared into his backyard. Harold ran four miles every morning and swam for a least an hour every Saturday and Sunday. Tomorrow, he thought, he'd give Ava another swimming lesson. He'd get Heidi to come in the water with them to keep the girl calm. He pictured his intern standing at the side of the pool watching them: Harold (more fit than she'd probably imagined), Harold's sexy wife, and Harold's beautiful child. He wasn't really so different from any other man with a young daughter—it wasn't supposed to feel any different than it did.

Harold walked back to the bedroom in just his boxer shorts. He stood at the foot of the bed and smiled at his wife and daughter. "OK," he said, "I have an idea. You and me, Ava, let's go to your room and read a nice long book. It's after ten, so this is a very generous offer," he said.

Ava stayed curled against her mother, her fingers in her mouth. She was blinking slowly, as if she were already half asleep. Harold could almost feel his own body in the bed, curled against Heidi the way Ava was.

"It's time," he said, but as he leaned toward her, Ava jumped up and pulled her fingers from her mouth; her other hand flew up into the air. "I have an idea," she said, waving her arm and bouncing on the bed. "You sleep in my bed! You be the baby and I'll be the Daddy!"

An image of the girl, sucking on his wife's breast, flashed in

Harold's mind. He looked at his wife, who was smiling now, and wondered if she still loved him as she did when they married.

"Good, good, good," his daughter chanted, as if it had already been agreed upon. She stood up on the bed and started to jump.

"It's too late for this," Harold managed to say. He had to say it again because his daughter was laughing, and he wasn't sure they'd heard him. When he said it a third time, the girl stopped jumping and turned to face him.

"I'm sleeping here," Ava said, hands on her hips, looking right into Harold's eyes. She was grinning and fearless, as if she and Harold were playing a game and she knew she was going to win.

Harold almost felt sorry for the girl when her mother took his side. "Go ahead," Heidi said to the girl now, "Go with your father."

Ava cried for another ten minutes after that, clinging to her mother, Harold sitting at the foot of the bed, his hand rubbing his wife's calf. When Ava finally quieted down, Heidi nodded to Harold, giving him permission to finally take the child to her bed.

He held her tightly in his arms, and she laid her wet cheek on his bare shoulder. He closed the door to his bedroom behind them—he didn't want Heidi to hear it if the girl started crying again, though Ava's body felt so limp in his arms he couldn't imagine she had the energy to start up again. She was basically asleep, he thought.

When he opened the door to her room, the hinges squeaked, and she was startled by the sound. Her whole body jerked awake, and then she was crying again. He leaned forward to put her into the bed, but she clung to him, Harold bent at the waist over the bed and Ava holding tight to him with her arms and legs. But as soon as he was upright again and hugging her, she was desperate to break free of him. "Put me down," she yelled, and then she said, more quietly, "I hate you."

Harold put his lips to his daughter's forehead and kissed her again and again as she twisted her neck to avoid his kisses. She was sweating and breathing hard, but he hugged her to his chest until he got her to calm down.

He sat on the bed with the girl in his lap. She'd clearly exhausted herself—it happened often; she'd be hysterical until just a second before she shut her eyes and fell asleep for the night.

Harold was exhausted too. He cradled her body for a minute more, then laid her on the mattress and tucked her under the covers. Still, she fought to keep her eyes open; her eyelids would start to close and then she'd pull them up again.

She was still half-awake when Harold leaned down, his mouth right over her ear. "I'm not your real father," he said. It was the only time in his life he said this to her, the only time she ever heard the truth.

Everything Nice

Two girls, Nora and Abigail, sit cross-legged on the concrete basement floor of Abigail's house. The girls are twelve years old. On the floor between them is a pack of cigarettes, a pack of matches, and two tall glasses of lemonade.

The walls of the basement are lined with boxes that are so worn items have begun to poke through the cardboard. Abigail's old baby carriage is parked under a small window at the back of the room, its canopy half-collapsed and a redheaded doll in its seat. Next to the carriage is a rusted toolbox; an axe leans up against it.

The space is dimly lit and dusty. It smells like metal and mildew.

Abigail's mother is in the kitchen upstairs, thinking that Abigail and Nora are at the park. The girls can hear her footsteps squeaking the floorboards above them.

There are three pimples on Abigail's chin, and Nora can't help but stare at them. The pimples are clustered together as if commiserating, and they're red because Abagail won't stop rubbing them.

"You look scared," Abigail says. "Why are you scared?"

"I'm not," Nora says, but she is scared—she just doesn't know why. Abigail's pimples make her look like a stranger, someone older and intimidating, but Nora isn't scared of Abigail because Abigail is really no different than she ever was. She still licks her lips before and after she takes a sip of her drink, and she still speaks very quickly, so she sounds a little bit panicked, even when she's not. Nora isn't afraid of smoking, and she's not scared of the basement. It's something else, something nebulous and bigger than any of these things.

But the idea of trying to explain this, even to Abigail, is exhausting. It would be like trying to describe what it feels like to be alive, to realize that you're alive and traveling into the future in every moment.

ʘ

Nora's sister Alison is seven years old. She's spending the day at her aunt's house. Her cousin, Billy, who's eleven, is giving her a tour of their swimming pool. They're not supposed to be in the pool without supervision, but Billy's mother has been taking more and more naps lately—Alison's mother calls this a definite sign of depression—and they were too hot and bored to wait. Besides, the pool looked so inviting, glimmering blue in the sunlight.

Alison holds onto Billy's back with her arms and legs wrapped around him. She's not a very good swimmer—if she doesn't hold on tight, she'll sink, or that's what it feels like, especially when Billy pulls her into the deep end.

But Alison is bold and adventurous. She is the captain of Billy, who is her own special boat. She lifts her chest from his back and watches his arms stretch forward, his hands meeting above his head and then moving arc-like down to his hips, pulling them through the water. His hair clings to his scalp as he swims, but when he slows down, the strands separate and float to the surface.

He breathes heavily when he lifts his head from the water, and Alison wonders what would happen if she pushed him back under and held him there. She pictures Aunt Ruth finding them curled like sleeping kittens at the bottom of the pool.

If Alison died in the pool, they'd plant a tree at her school and place a plaque with her name at its base, just like they did for David Lakoff when he rode his bike into oncoming traffic.

ᘓ

Abigail takes two cigarettes from the pack and hands one to Nora. Neither of them has smoked before, and Nora feels clumsy holding the cigarette between two fingers. She pictures the high school boys who smoke behind the playground at her school. Nora will never feel that old; she knows this. Even when she's thirty she'll feel like an imposter, a child playing dress up.

When Abigail lights a match, it smells like a campfire. It smells like Christmas. This is the way Nora imagines that God must smell.

By the second cigarette, they learn how to pull smoke into their lungs and hold it there, to let their lungs burn and do nothing about it.

Nora feels shy with Abigail as she watches her smoke, until Abigail opens just the corners of her mouth and blows smoke in two steady streams from the sides of her face. Then the two of them laugh and everything is normal again.

"Did I tell you my dad used to be a chain-smoker?" Abigail asks. She lifts the cigarette to her lips and inhales. "Mom tells everyone he quit for her because she wasn't about to marry a smoker, but he didn't completely quit, and let's just say Mom knows it. One time, he was away at this conference and had like one cigarette—he walks through the door two days later, and Mom goes, *You smoked!*"

There is something hypnotizing about Abigail's story, the way she's talking about smoking and smoking at the same time. Nora's head feels heavier. Her eyes are beginning to burn.

"Last time," Abigail says, but then she stops talking.

Smoke pools in the air between them. Nora thinks she can hear the sound of it in the silence, a low-pitched buzz. It feels like a lot of time is passing, Nora staring at Abigail's lower lip until she thinks she can see it throbbing. It seems like such a long time that Nora wonders if Abigail already finished her story and somehow Nora missed the ending.

But then Abigail takes a sip of her drink, licks her lips, and says, "So Mom goes, *Get in the f-ing car*, and she drives him like ten miles from the house—windows wide open so he wouldn't stink up her car. And this was the middle of winter, I'll have you know. Snowing, like blizzard snowing." Abigail blows smoke at the ceiling, as if aiming it at her mother upstairs. "So we drop him on the side of this random road, and Mom makes him run home. She said he smelled like crap and the only way to get rid of that smell was to sweat it out. He did it too," Abigail says. She smiles just slightly as she lifts the cigarette to her mouth. This time, when she takes a drag, it sounds like a kiss.

"I like how they smell," Nora says. She puts the cigarette to her lips and tries to make the kissing sound, but she can't do it.

"I'm starting to feel dizzy," Abigail says. She grinds the tip of her cigarette into the floor and lies on her back.

It's warm in the basement, and Nora's shirt clings to her. As she watches Abigail's chest rise and fall, she imagines both of their bodies swelling until they fill the basement entirely.

CR

Alison holds onto Billy's shoulders as he moves in slow circles around the deep end of the pool. She keeps forgetting that she knows how to swim—she can't swim as well as Billy, but she could swim to the edge or even the shallow end if she had to.

The pool is fenced, and around the fence there are trees. Alison pictures herself at the center of the world, in her own private bath. Billy is her servant and her carrier.

"Swim faster," she tells him, but Billy slows down instead and then stops. His body shimmies in place as he treads water under the shade of the diving board. He doesn't feel like a boat when he's not swimming; he feels slippery and hard to hold onto.

"Grab the diving board," Billy says, "You're too heavy," but Alison doesn't think she can reach it—not until Billy takes her wrist and lifts her arm in the air and the next thing she knows, she has the board in her hand. She wraps her fingers around its scratchy edge, reaches up with her other arm and holds on tight.

She likes hanging this way, until Billy grabs on too and the board begins to wobble. They're face-to-face, hanging from opposite sides of the platform. "Don't fall," Billy says, and he laughs, shaking the board on purpose now.

Alison can see muscles and tendons moving in Billy's neck as he wobbles the board. His hair is slicked back and the inside corners of his eyes look red. "Now grab onto me," he says. When he lets go of the board it shakes harder, but Alison doesn't let go. "Come on," Billy says, "Hug onto me."

Alison wants to stay where she is, hanging from the board, but her arms and fingers are starting to burn. She wants to say, *Just grab me*, but instead she says, "I can swim by myself."

She makes it to the shallow end on her own, half swimming, half pulling herself along the wall, and she's gasping for air once she stops. She got water in her nose and it feels like it's burning her brain.

Meanwhile, Billy is summersaulting underwater. He pays no attention to Alison. Even when his feet kick water in her direction, he's not splashing her on purpose.

Alison waits and watches. When Billy stands on his hands and holds his pink feet still above the water, she tickles his toes until he comes up laughing.

"The best part is now," he says. He pulls Alison by the wrist to the side of the pool. Then he guides her hand in his along the concrete wall until both of their hands are pushed to the center of the pool and then up to the surface by water that shoots hard and fast from a small hole.

They both try to hold their hands over the hole, but Billy is better at this—Alison's hand is pushed away so easily, like it has no strength at all. She wants to keep trying, but Billy tells her to move. He has something else to show her.

With his feet and calves resting on the pavement and his knees bent over the edge of the pool, Billy drops his butt down into the water so that it must be pushed right against the hole. His head is underwater; little bubbles float up from his nose. Alison watches him, repeating his phrase in her head: *The best part is now, the best part is now.*

෪

Abigail is still lying on her back on the floor. Her eyes are closed. Nora leans down to check on her, and she can smell Abigail's shampoo, the cigarettes and lemonade on her breath.

Then Abigail reaches up and pulls Nora into a hug on the floor. Nora can feel Abigail's left hip bone against her stomach, the rise and fall of Abigail's rib cage.

She tries to rest as little of her weight as possible on Abigail, but she feels dizzy too now that she's lying down. It feels like the blood in her brain has somehow carbonated, turned fizzy like soda.

With Abigail's arms around her, all Nora can do to get space to breathe is lift her head. When she does, she can see Abigail's face up close, the little white dot at the center of each pimple on her chin, the way the pimples stretch her skin. And Nora kisses them, as if they're bruises: one little kiss for each pimple.

Abigail hugs her tighter then, and Nora lowers her head back down so they're cheek to cheek. They adjust their bodies so their legs alternate against the floor: Abigail's then Nora's, Abigail's then Nora's.

It's hard for Nora to catch her breath, but the more she tries to quiet her breathing—she doesn't want Abigail to hear it—the harder it is to breathe at all.

Then, through the small window just above them, they hear a car in the driveway, Abigail's mother driving away. They can hear the sound of the engine and the tires rolling on the pavement. Nora thinks about long drives in the dark, drifting off to sleep in the backseat.

When she repositions herself just slightly, Abigail shifts under her, lifting her hips and then lowering them. Abigail presses her body into Nora's, lifting and lowering her hips again and again. Then Abigail's hand is between their legs, and Nora is mimicking Abigail's movements.

They make sounds that Nora doesn't recognize as theirs, animal sounds, or it sounds like they're in pain, but it doesn't feel like pain, not exactly.

And as they're doing this, Nora thinks of a story she heard about a woman who rubbed peanut butter between her legs and let her dog lick it off. She tries to force this image out of her mind, but it keeps coming back. Meanwhile, her head and chest feel like they're burning, like they're bright red.

Then she feels Abigail's body shudder, and she jumps to her feet. "I'm sorry," Nora says, "Did I hurt you?"

Abigail doesn't answer. She stands up and she looks at Nora for only a second, then she's running upstairs.

Nora's not sure what to do. She looks around the room, searching, and sees the doll in the carriage, so she takes it and holds it in her lap. She braids and unbraids the doll's red hair, over and over, not knowing what else to do.

ભ

Billy pulls himself out of the pool and sits on the edge with his feet in the water. "Do you see this?" he says, pointing at his lap. "The water hole makes my dick big."

Alison feels stuck in place, like she can't move. Without thinking, she says, "Can I touch it?"

"No way," Billy says. "Are you crazy? You can't touch my dick."

"Don't call it that!" Alison says, splashing her arms in the water. "Just stop talking to me."

Billy slips back into the pool. He dips his chin and lower lip under the water so that the bottom half of his smile appears to wobble and stretch.

"Can I try it?" Alison asks.

"You can't," Billy says. "You don't have a dick." He tilts his head back and spits a stream of water out of his mouth and up into the air.

"I don't need one to do it," Alison says. "I don't even want a gross dick."

She knows she won't be able to hang from her legs, so she stands on her toes in front of the hole and lifts herself up into the air, hands flat on the side of the pool. Warm water rushes between her legs, making that whole area begin to tingle.

"You're disgusting," Billy says. "You're like five years old."

"I'm seven," Alison says. She bounces off her toes and spreads her legs.

"Come on, stop that," Billy says.

Alison ignores him, but she can feel that he's watching her. She lifts herself higher, spreads her legs farther apart. The sun is a spotlight on her forehead.

"You know what's going to happen?" Billy asks.

"Nothing," Alison says. She doesn't look at Billy, who's standing right at her side.

"That water's going to get into your vagina," he tells her. "It's going to fill you up and then you'll puff out like crazy."

"You're stupid," Alison says, but she lifts herself a little bit higher so that the water is hitting her lower in the legs. She stays that way until her arms ache and she can't hold herself anymore.

"You're actually gross," Billy says. He turns and swims away from her.

Alison leans against the side of the pool and watches Billy swim. The sun is behind her. It feels like an electric blanket draped over her shoulders. Cool water laps at her ribs and under her arms. She rubs her toes against a rough spot at the bottom of the pool. "Come be my boat," she calls to Billy, but he doesn't hear her.

Then clouds pass in front of the sun and everything gets darker.

There is a cool breeze, and Alison's blanket is gone. Half-dead leaves fall from the trees into the pool. No one in the whole entire world can see me, she thinks.

ൟ

Twenty minutes after she left, Abigail comes back to the basement. She's changed her clothes and her hair is wet.

"You're still here?" she says to Nora. She lifts her left foot, points her toes, and draws an invisible circle on the floor. "You need to see something," she says.

She turns around and lifts the back of her shirt almost to her shoulders. There is a series of blotches along her spine, where her skin looks raw and red.

"Do you see that?" Abigail looks over her shoulder at Nora. "You hurt me," she says. "I won't tell, but I wanted you to see what you did."

Nora's hands and feet feel huge and heavy. She doesn't know what to say. She just stands there. Her fingertips and toes start to tingle.

"You can't do that kind of thing," Abigail says, facing Nora now. "I tried to push you off and I couldn't."

"You didn't," Nora says, which feels like the truth until, a second later, it doesn't. "I didn't do anything," she says. She pictures her own body on top of Abigail's, pinning her down and pushing against her, Abigail's back scraping against the floor. She thinks of the dog again, of the peanut butter. Then she thinks of her mother for a second, pictures her thick black hair and the way she looks when she smiles.

"You're sweating," Abigail says. "I can see it on your face."

"It's hot," Nora says. "I hate the summer. You know that." She pulls at her shirt. It's clinging, and she can't stand the feeling of it. "Do you want to keep the cigarettes?" she asks.

Abigail rolls her eyes. "They made me sick," she says. "You saw."

That's when Nora notices the three dots of blood on Abigail's chin, right where her pimples had been. "You're bleeding," she says, but Abigail just stands there with her hands on her hips. "Right there," Nora clarifies, pointing, and Abigail squints her eyes into slits.

∽

Alison pulls at the front of her bathing suit until it balloons with air. She presses her pregnant belly against the side of the pool to pop it and then re-inflates.

"Now what are you doing?" Billy asks.

"Nothing," Alison says. She pulls at the leg hole of her bathing suit until her balloon deflates.

"You know you're weird?" Billy says. He dips his head forward and flips it back, throwing water from his hair into Alison's face.

The water stings her eyes; her body is beginning to feel cold and tired. She pictures herself stuck in the pool forever, the water getting colder and colder until finally Aunt Ruth throws the winter tarp over top and traps Alison underneath. "I don't want to swim anymore," she tells Billy.

"So, get out," he says. He flips onto his back and floats next to her with his eyes closed.

"I don't feel well," she tells him. "I want to go home." She has to pull at his arm to get him to stop floating and look at her. "I really don't feel good," she says.

"What's the matter?" Billy asks, but Alison doesn't know how to answer his question. It feels like the water is spicy with chemicals, like it's invading her body. "Are you crying?" Billy asks.

"It's the chlorine," she says. "I have water and chlorine everywhere."

"Please don't cry," Billy says. He puts his hand on her arm but she pulls it away.

"I think the water got inside me," she tells him.

"It didn't," Billy says, but she feels it, a growing bubble of water in her belly. "I was only kidding," Billy says. "You're okay. I promise you're okay. Please don't cry, Allie."

"I'm not," she says, but she is crying, even though she's trying as hard as she can not to.

"Maybe some water is trapped in your bathing suit," Billy says. "Maybe that's why it hurts, but it will come out, real easy."

Alison pictures the bubble of water hiding inside her for days. When she's at camp, playing archery or dodge ball, it'll slip out and leave a big wet stain on the seat of her shorts. "I need to get it out now," she says. Although, in truth, she doesn't feel anything anymore. No pain, no bubble.

"Hold onto the side of the pool," Billy tells her. He stands behind her and puts his hand on her lower back. Alison presses her stomach to the wall. "Spread your legs," he tells her.

She assumes he's going to tap her back until the water comes out, but then she feels his hand between her legs. She feels his finger hook around the edge of her bathing suit and pull the material to the side, from one thigh to the other.

Alison can feel the water right against the folds of her skin, and it feels colder there than anywhere else. It's actually a nice feeling.

"Okay," Billy says, and then she feels his finger poking at her. She feels a sharp pain, his finger pushing its way inside, and she jerks forward.

When her nose hits the edge of the pool, she hears a thud, but she doesn't feel any pain; it's just numb. Her whole face feels numb and puffy and warm. Little flecks of light float in the air in front of her.

She isn't scared until she wipes her nose with her hand and sees the blood. That's when she reaches for Billy. Her arms stretch out and she leans forward, but he's moved out of reach.

"Get out of the pool," he yells at her, but Alison just stands there, crying as hard as she can—until she realizes that it doesn't really hurt; it's still mostly numb.

Alison stands in the pool and watches drops of blood fall from her face, hitting the surface of the water, staying drop-like for only a second and then spreading and turning the water pink.

"Get out," Billy is yelling, but Alison wants to stay right where she is.

Her nose is starting to ache and her top lip is tingling, but mostly she's just interested: her insides dripping out of her body and into the water—she's never seen anything quite like it.

The Twins

A woman gives birth to a set of twins: one is skinny and blue-eyed, its whole self tiny and blue-tinged; the other one has black eyes and dark skin and is very fat.

The woman holds the blue one and loves it. She wants to hug it so tight she has to stop herself because she's sure she could crush this little skinny one. *I made a little skinny one!* she thinks, and she feels almost weightless, like she could soar through the air and impress everyone below.

The skinny baby bats its eyelashes and squeezes the woman's thumb with its skinny fingers. The fat one is in the cabinet in the next room. The woman keeps thinking she hears that big baby crying, but when she holds perfectly still and listens, she can't hear anything but the wind blowing at her windows.

This cabinet is made up of many small square compartments, each with its own small wooden door. In this cabinet the woman stores the odds and ends she is not ready to discard but wants out of her sight. These odds and ends are carefully organized in the cabinet, but the woman emptied and disinfected the bottom left compartment for her twins.

"I'm sorry for leaving you in here so long," she tells the fat one when she takes him out of the cabinet. She presses her lips to her big baby's warm, plushy cheek. The skinny one is so skinny the woman has to swaddle her in multiple pink blankets and cradle her in pillows so she doesn't roll around in the compartment and bruise herself, except then the woman thinks about that, how cute and lovable the skinny one would look with bruises. So she removes most of the pillows and un-swaddles the skinny one and closes the cabinet door, and that too feels like love, almost like she's on the brink of loving herself.

The fat baby is already smiling. If this fat one belonged to someone else, the woman would probably think he was beautiful. Her fat baby has the sort of presence that strikes you, that is powerful, but this isn't what the woman believes a baby should be. It's not in a baby's best interest to be healthy and strong like this. Every time she looks at the pudgy folds on his little thighs she feels like crying. She feels like pushing her nails into them. Then she pictures his wounds pus-filled and repulsive to anyone who sees them.

It's her smile, she realizes—the fat baby's face is just like hers. This is the smile she has hated in every photograph anyone's taken of her. She could explain every inch of this ugly face that she detests in particular, and she could explain why. But it's also the face she had when she was just a little girl, and sometimes, when she looks in the mirror, she's able to see that little thing she once was. In this way, her face sometimes looks beautiful, but only if she holds it just so. The problem is that she can't make this fat one hold its face just so. She tries. She twists the baby and holds it in such a way, but it keeps smiling at her like those photographs.

The woman exchanges the fat one for the skinny one. The skinny one is not yet smiling and in fact seems to have almost the inverse of a smile on its face. Not a frown, just an emptiness that the woman also recognizes as her own. When she pulls her thumb from the skinny baby's fist, its eyes grow wider and the bright blue color of them drains. It's a ridiculous, pathetic way to ask for love. "No one will ever love you as you want to be loved, so you might as well cut the crap," the woman says to the skinny baby. She wants to eat this skinny baby and then kill herself—she has this instinct, but she's too tired to do it.

She puts the skinny one in the cabinet with the fat one. It requires shoving. Their two heads collide, this hollow-sounding, terrible thunk. She has to push the cabinet door very hard until it clicks closed, until they're smashed in there together and she leaves them to duke it out. The winner will be mine, she thinks, and I will love the winner so much. Everyone loves a winner.

When she opens the cabinet two days later, it appears there is only one baby in there. The one baby has blue eyes and skinny limbs and its belly is huge, but it's not one baby, she realizes—it's both babies together. The skinny one ate the fat one. The skin of it is pink, almost red, blushing all over, like every cell is brimming with shame. *I have to start over*, the woman thinks. *This is in no way acceptable.*

She decides she can let them live as long as she doesn't have to witness it. She takes the babies outside and lays them on the grass. The sun is setting and it will be dark soon. She hears a train passing in the distance. "Go," she says to her babies. She doesn't look back, not even when they start to whimper and then rage behind her. Instead, the woman looks through the window into her living room, which is beautifully lit, warm and inviting and quiet and all hers.

Later she goes into the backyard expecting them to be gone, hoping they're gone the way you hope that a mistake you've made was only made in a dream, but there they are, the fat one a more prominent lump inside the skinny one's belly. "I guess you don't want to live," the woman says, not surprised by this realization but still sad about it.

She digs a hole in the ground with her hands, cutting and chapping her skin in the process. Later, she'll look at the scrapes on her knuckles and the dirt under her broken nails and she'll think about how irresponsible she is. She'll bandage her own hands and cry for her own pain the way she should really have bandaged and cried for her children. She'll rub thick antiseptic on her cuts. She'll scrub and trim and file her broken nails. She'll wrap her hands with bandages and tape them carefully in place. She'll give them gentle kisses when they ache. She'll whisper to her knuckles, *I love you, I promise to take better care of you.*

In her lawn, in no spot in particular, she has buried the bulbous, blue-eyed baby with the dark baby inside it. "I'm sorry I made you and then I couldn't love you," she said to them sincerely.

Later, she returns to the backyard to mourn. She thinks her fat baby would have grown up to love the roses she grows on the trellis in her front yard, so she pulls down fistfuls for him. For her skinny baby she steals white lilies from her neighbor, who would have to understand, given the circumstances. Who wouldn't be willing to sacrifice some lilies for a skinny dead baby? Of course the woman's skinny baby is no longer really skinny, but she was born skinny, and that has to be worth something.

A pure, comforting sadness washes over the woman as she carries the red and white flowers through her yard in the middle of the night. As the wind throws dried leaves at her ankles, the woman searches for the exact place where she buried her babies. She feels a desperate love for them in these moments. She imagines her little babies cooing in her arms, one tucked cozy inside the other, but she's a little bit relieved when she remembers they're dead and buried.

When she does find the grave, the woman sees that there's a skinny pink arm sticking up from the ground, as if raising its hand in school. Specks of dirt cling to it. Without thinking, the woman drops the flowers and pushes her bandaged thumb into the small hand, but there's no grasping instinct left in her babies. It's like a slap to the chest: she feels and doesn't feel the tight snugness of her baby's little hand holding her, the warm fist of her daughter that had always clutched her finger until now. Kneeling on the ground in the middle of the night, her thumb ungrasped, the woman feels like someone has drilled a sphere of ice through her ribs, jamming it between her heart and left lung.

She wipes the arm clean with rose petals and then tries to tickle it, but her baby's arm is like a little tree trunk that has lost its leaves and sits sadly in winter, waiting stoically for spring. The woman kisses the arm. She wants to open her mouth and suck on her poor baby's arm, but the arm is rotting and the smell and taste of it are sickening.

"I've made a huge mess," she says. She lifts her chin to the sky and looks up at the stars and wonders how other women manage to give birth to babies and care for them and let them grow. How do these women produce living babies and just let them grow into whatever they want to grow into? How can they handle the pain and the love of it all? "It doesn't matter," she tells herself. "I can always try again." But she's still holding onto that little arm.

This is my mess, she thinks, and she picks up a stick and slaps at the arm. *If you make this kind of mess, you have no choice but to clean it up.* She slaps and slaps with the stick, but the arm doesn't move. With two hands, she manages to bend the arm into an arc like a bridge, the tiny fingers pointed to the ground. Her baby's skin is rotting, but she can't help kissing it, even as she presses her palms into the curved bone at the top of the bridge and lifts her knees from the ground, using all of her weight to drive it down. As the last bit of arm is submerged, the woman is on her knees again, her face to the ground, her lips on her babies and then pressed to nothing but soil. When she finally lifts her head, the ice in her chest begins to melt and then burn, a trickle of burning hot water raking through her.

For the rest of the night the woman stares at the stretch of empty wall just beside the cabinet. She sees her son as a man, tall, dark, and handsome, building houses with his hands and painting beautiful pictures of men swimming in the sea. This man, her son, is a white-coat-wearing doctor who takes care of her when she's old. Then she pictures her pale daughter in a bikini, lying stupidly in the sun until her skin is puffy and red, a Save Me sign nailed to her belly. But then she pictures her daughter as an airplane pilot, soaring high above the ground, serious and powerful and free. Her babies really could have been something.

As the night passes and train after train runs in the distance, the woman sits in her rocking chair with her arms held just above her lap, as if cradling her babies, one in each arm. She kisses the cold air—one, two—as if kissing their foreheads. She squeezes her arms around her own body, as if crushing the babies to her.

As the woman's arms and eyelids grow heavy and she feels herself falling to sleep, she sees her grown babies holding her in their strong hands, their arms stretched above their heads, marching her through the world this way. "Our mother," they would have said, parading her, "this is our mother."

The Triplets

B ecause the doctor is a doctor, the woman on the exam table is naked from the waist down. She tucks her heels into the metal holsters at the foot of the table, lets her knees fall into butterfly position, then slides her bare bottom toward the doctor, who sits on a stool between the woman's legs.

"Good," the doctor says.

The doctor has long gray hair and fleshy arms covered in wrinkles that look like lace. Her shirt on this day is yellow, roomy, and sleeveless. She wears navy workpants and black sneakers.

The woman has seen this doctor in the past, but those visits were routine, unremarkable. The doctor probably said, *Looking good! See you next year!* then moved onto her next patient.

This time, the woman and the doctor had a brief chat before the exam. The woman said, "Hi, how are you?" and the doctor said, "Good!" her voice springy, as if she were surprised and delighted to be asked.

Then the doctor looked at the woman's chart. "Well, you're not good. You've been bleeding for two months." She skipped the usual question about sexual partners, as if, this time, the answer was obvious: zero.

It was the nurse who told the woman to remove her underwear and any blood-catching devices she had inside her.

"Stunning day out there. Right?" the doctor says. Her office is downtown, but next to the city's biggest park. The woman can see the leafy green of it through the window.

As the doctor inserts the speculum, the woman reminds herself that this doctor chose to be a doctor. She could have been a park ranger or elementary school teacher.

It's not as if the woman picked a passenger on the bus and said, *Hey! Would you look in my vagina to see if it looks diseased and/or disgusting? I'm going to spread my legs as wide as I can and slide my backside toward you. Watch out for blood!*

She worries that she made the appointment prematurely. What if she took the spot from someone who's disabled or poverty-stricken and/or about to give birth?

One lady, in her online review, said the doctor was "accommodating." That's all she wrote. Her username was NeedyBlakKat.

Blood gushes when the doctor removes the speculum. "Oosh," she says.

"Sorry," the woman replies.

Vagina, she repeated to herself on the bus to the doctor's office. She told herself it wasn't her fault—she was born with this part. There's nothing shameful about it. No doctor had ever said, *Whoa! Your vagina? You want me to look in your vagina?*

If anyone who'd seen hers thought it was particularly weird or off-putting, they hadn't said so. There's no reason to think it had become weird or off-putting, except that it wouldn't stop bleeding.

"You have fibroids," the doctor says. "They're huge. That's why you're bleeding so much."

What's a fibroid, exactly? the woman wants to ask, but fibroid sounds too much like fiber. The fact that she and the doctor both have long tubes of poop inside them—and vaginas—is not comforting.

"Can you take them out?" the woman asks. "I don't want to have them."

"That's understandable," the doctor laughs, revealing teeth so crooked they look like they've turned toward each other to commiserate. She gets up from her stool and returns to the counter where she left the chart.

"Should I get dressed?" the woman asks.

"That's strange," the doctor says. She's holding the chart in her bare left hand. Her other hand is still gloved, and the woman's blood is on that glove. It's flattering—the fact that she's still wearing it.

"You know what?" the doctor says. "I don't think those are fibroids I felt. I want to get a better look in there."

"You want to?"

She dims the lights and pulls the ultrasound machine from the corner.

"Do you feel powerful?" the woman asks.

"This is on wheels. It's very easy to move." The doctor shifts the machine back and forth as if to illustrate.

"I mean, in general, out in the world?"

"Sometimes," the doctor says cheerfully.

"But you can save lives. Do you ever sit on the bus and think, *If anything happens to my fellow passengers, I could open them up and fix them?*"

"I think we're all pretty powerful. Think of the bus driver," she says, slipping a plastic covering onto the probe. She gives the woman a closed-lip smile as she rubs lubricant all over it. She's still wearing the bloody glove.

The woman's mother is a nurse. She likes to say, *I take care of patients' hearts and nerves. I make them feel cared for and safe.* But she can't save lives.

In fact, the woman has a recurrent dream in which her mother finds someone who is hurt and dying and can't do anything about it. Often, in the dream, her mother can't reach the sufferer, not even to offer comfort. In her favorite version of the dream, doctors are there. Sometimes they arrive after the patient has died, so they take care of the woman and her mother because they're grieving. In her most favorite version, which she only experienced once, her mother has a heart attack—when the doctors arrive, they tend to the woman's mother instead of the suffering patient.

"You'll need a full bladder for the external scan," the doctor says,

"So you'll have to come back. This won't hurt," she says, holding the long probe like a lightsaber.

Instinctively, the woman squeezes her thighs together, but the doctor says, "Uh uh. Open up."

It reminds the woman of her childhood dentist, who always said, *Open big, big!*

"You're not disgusted by blood and disease?" she asks.

The doctor laughs again. "Are you kidding? Blood and disease are my bread and butter."

The woman closes her eyes. She pictures the doctor with a napkin tucked into her shirt as she wipes the blood from her glove onto a slice of pumpernickel, adds avocado and onion powder, taking her first bite while sitting on her stool between the woman's spread-apart thighs.

What would her dentist have said if she had vagina blood on her teeth? Not *Open big, big!* that's for sure.

The doctor rests her bare hand on the woman's knee. "Breathe," she says, then takes a big, audible breath herself.

Why do I feel so weird all the time? the woman wants to ask. *Does everyone?* Instead, she says, "I want to be your patient." She didn't mean to say it.

"You are my patient." The doctor has many patients, but maybe she doesn't use this exact smile on all of them. Maybe she hasn't used it on any of them ever. Maybe she hasn't given this exact smile to anyone else in the whole world.

She makes a humming sound as she pushes the ultrasound probe inside the woman's body. She moves it like it's part of her: an extra, magical limb.

"Okay," the doctor says, stretching the word. "Okay," she says again, even slower, looking at the screen.

The woman imagines herself bicycling down a suburban street, the doctor's steadying grip on the handlebar. *You're doing it!* the doctor says. *You're a normal, bicycling human!* She pictures the wheels of the bicycle spinning and spinning, one behind each of her eyeballs.

"Well, well," the doctor says. "Okay. I know why you're bleeding so much." Her head is framed by the woman's legs. "You have three very small hearts in there." She looks the woman in the eye. "They're beating away. Releasing blood like it's going out of style. I want to see you back here tomorrow. You win the prize for most compelling case, that's for sure."

There's a suction sound when she pulls out the probe. The woman sits up on the table.

"Slow movements," the doctor instructs. "No fainting, you hear? I need to get a blood count. I'll send in the nurse. Hold tight, okay?"

Once, the woman had a doctor who drew her blood himself. It was like having Ronald McDonald cook her fries.

☙

As she walks from the doctor's office to the bus stop, she feels a spring in her step, spring like the season, the way the world comes alive; she's more aware of all that is living around her, but inside her too: a spark that is uniquely hers.

The dizziness is connected to the doctor, so it feels safe, like there's an invisible net that moves with her. It feels so wonderful to be caught—it's worth falling for that, to have someone who is interested in catching you. If she weren't dizzy, she wouldn't have that, wouldn't deserve it.

☙

When she gets home, the woman lies on the couch and calls her mother at work.

"What do you mean three little hearts?" her mother asks.

The woman hears muffled words paged over the loudspeaker at the hospital, some important announcement almost everyone is meant to ignore.

"The doctor found three beating hearts in my uterus," she says.

"So you're pregnant with triplets? Now I know you're kidding."

The woman explains what the doctor said, that the hearts are pumping her own blood out of her body.

"This makes absolutely no sense," her mother says.

"My doctor's never seen it before either."

"Hearts? You have three hearts pumping blood out of your body? Are you trying to be cute?"

"My doctor said I'm severely anemic because of it."

Her mother groans. "Don't tell me you've gone vegan again."

When the woman was young, any problem she had, she went to the hospital where her mother was head nurse, beloved by patients, doctors, and administrators. The woman was treated like a VIP from the moment she was born in their emergency room during one of her mother's shifts.

"Plenty of healthy people are vegan," the woman says.

"And you're not doing anything else you shouldn't be doing?"

"I haven't in a long time," the woman says.

"Have you been using the scar cream I gave you?"

"I will," the woman says.

She hears her mother exhale. "I work with the best gyno in the city. Why don't you call him?"

When the woman went to college out of state, she saw doctors who kept their distance, treated her with respect, but not special care. She preferred this. She didn't want to cut the line, accept VIP status she didn't need or deserve.

"Who is this doctor you saw?" her mother is asking.

"She's my doctor. I like her."

"And what did this doctor give you for the anemia?"

"She's putting a team together. They haven't come up with a treatment plan yet."

"How about treating yourself to a hamburger?"

❧

When she gets off the phone, she calls the doctor's office. She feels disgusting, like those hearts are rotting, buck-toothed, hairy tumors, super-sized by her vegan diet.

"Are you a patient?" the receptionist asks.

"I was just there. I need to talk to the doctor."

"So you need to make an appointment."

"I'd like to speak with the doctor. If she's not busy. It's just, I'm bleeding a lot."

"Are you pregnant?" the receptionist asks.

"Could I talk to the doctor?"

"She's with a patient. If this is an emergency, you need to call 911."

"I just have a quick question. She told me something, and I think I misunderstood."

"I can take your number and have her call you back, but she's with patients all afternoon."

CR

They can't be real hearts, she realizes. The doctor said that to be nice, because the woman couldn't even handle the idea of fibroids, which, according to the internet, are very common and have nothing to do with dietary fiber.

Maybe she is anemic, and that's made her confused, so she didn't properly understand what the doctor said. She's overestimated the doctor's interest. She's fine. As fine as anyone, as ordinary.

In fact, when she goes to the bathroom to check on the bleeding, she finds nothing. Before she left the doctor's office she reinserted two different blood-catching devices and used a big pad. She was sure she'd soaked through it all.

Yet there's part of her that continues to believe in the hearts.

As a teenager, when she was in treatment for an eating disorder, she learned about interoception, how to listen to the inside of her body. If she could hear what it needed, feel it, her own hunger and fullness, her need for rest, her breath, her heartbeat, she could take care of it, respond to its needs. It seemed stupid then, a bad idea—her body was mad and greedy; if she listened to it, who knows where she'd end up.

Now she doesn't feel that way. Her favorite part of the day is at the end, when she wears ear plugs and listens to her heartbeat as she lies in bed. She likes to imagine that she's an orphaned animal, her own heart a comforting approximation of her missing mother's beating heart, her hands warm water bottles, an approximation of her missing mother's body. She is comforter and comforted: a closed system.

Now, still on the toilet, she presses her palms to her ears. She can hear the heart in her chest, but that's it.

She pictures her mother at work, worried for no reason. She pictures the doctor with her long gray hair. Who keeps their hair so long at that age? How old is the doctor anyway?

At the eating disorder treatment center, they told her: *Stop fighting your body. Accept the things you cannot change. Surrender.* She didn't take that advice. Her plan was to take it eventually—it was obviously good advice. In the meantime, she liked testing her body, seeing how much it could take.

Recently, she scratched an itch on her arm and it grew bumps in protest. When she scratched the bumps, they released liquid the color of apple juice.

If you scratch, it's going to itch more, her mother used to say, but it's not true—not if you scratched so hard you bled. Even the liquid-filled bumps felt more painful than itchy after she'd scratched hard enough.

What about the hearts? Were they part of her? If they were hurting, would she feel it?

She decides to conduct a test with a pair of long-blade scissors. If there are no little hearts inside her, the test will produce no pain or blood. She can keep the blades closed, stick both inside her without accidentally cutting anything. If she feels some resistance or starts to bleed, then maybe, not definitely, the doctor is right and her mother is wrong, not that she wants her mother to be wrong.

The test fails. Produces no blood. She's fine. There's nothing wrong with her. She needs to eat meat. She needs to take care of herself instead of forcing others to do it.

She's going to try the test again, use a different tool, but her roommate comes home. "I'm just here to get my skates," she calls to the woman, who is still in the bathroom. "Do you want to come to the park? It's a beautiful day. Are you in the bathroom?" she says, knocking.

"I had my appointment," the woman says. It was her roommate who had encouraged her to go to the doctor, insisted, but now she seems to have forgotten. "The doctor told me to rest," the woman says, as way of reminder.

When she comes out of the bathroom, she tells her roommate about the hearts, omitting the fact that she is no longer bleeding.

"My gosh," her roommate says. "What do you think it means?"

"I don't know," the woman says.

"Do you think it's a sign? A symbol? I know a woman who wanted a baby so badly she developed a symbolic pregnancy. She had every symptom, except a fetus."

"I really don't want a baby," the woman says.

"But maybe it's something like that. You feel okay? You look pale."

Usually, it's her roommate who seems special. When she published her first poetry book with a major press, the critics said her poems were *literary sunshine*.

"Fluff," the roommate says, "What time is?" She's meeting her boyfriend to skate—she hadn't mentioned that. "Rest. I'll bring you a treat."

The woman shouldn't be mad at her roommate for leaving. She should join her, actually, go to the park. Enjoy the day. Have a burger. Be normal. Have fun. Move on. Take care of herself.

She doesn't want to poke or aggravate the hearts. She doesn't want to hurt them.

The woman gets into bed, plugs her ears. And, magic: one big heartbeat, followed by three small heartbeats. *We're here, we're here together, with you.*

When she wakes up the next morning, she can only hear two little hearts beating. She has a vague memory of poking the hearts in the middle of the night, but she's not sure if it really happened. She also remembers using something to try to grab them—tweezers, she thinks, but then she remembers: spaghetti tongs.

She's sure it was a dream until she gets to the bathroom and finds the bloody tongs on the floor and, tucked under the bathmat, a single heart, limp and tiny.

She leaves it there to check on the others. Relieved, she finds the other two must be picking up the slack—her menstrual cup is so full it's overflowed, the two tampons and pad soaked.

She's still afraid to touch the heart on the floor, so she lifts it with the tongs.

Maybe it's the fan, or her eyes, or the dizziness, but it seems to be moving, slightly.

She fills the sink with water, not too hot or cold, no soap. And when she drops it in? The heart pumps and pumps, slowly at first, then with vigor. *You're doing it!* she says.

But the heart makes a groaning sound.

She can't leave it in the sink. What would her roommate think, not to mention her roommate's boyfriend. Her little heart is not a sign or symbol. It exists and wants to be inside her.

So she fills the menstrual cup with water and drops it in. The heart seems even happier, flipping as it pumps.

Kiss, kiss, she says, and reinserts the menstrual cup.

She takes a different route to the bus to the get to doctor's office. Usually she goes the long way, so she can pass the small hospital in her neighborhood, where white-coated doctors stand in the courtyard and drink their morning coffee. But today, she doesn't need to because she has her own doctor, who wants to see her, who knows her now.

◌ଃ

When she gets to the office, there are three small children sitting arm-to-arm on the one couch in the waiting room, a girl, a boy, and another girl, all blonde with green eyes.

The boy has freckles. "Hi," he says to the woman when she sits down. "Are you sick?"

"Not really," she says. From her desk, the receptionist looks at the woman and smiles.

"Are you having a baby?" the boy asks.

"I don't think so," the woman says, quieter this time.

"Our surrogate is pregnant," the smaller girl says. "Do you know what that means?"

"We're triplets," the bigger girl says, "But we're just getting one this time."

"A boy," the boy says.

"You don't know that," the girls say.

"I do know that," he says to the woman.

"He can be anything he wants," the smaller girl says, looking at her sister.

"That's a nice way to think about it," the woman says.

"It's not nice," the boy pouts.

For the first time since she left her apartment, the woman can feel all three hearts pumping. She pictures them sitting together on the couch, across from but still connected to her, beating in unison, the damaged one in the middle.

"We're getting frozen yogurt after this," the boy says.

A blonde, green-eyed man pokes his head out of the door that leads to the hallway that leads to the exam rooms. "Y'all okay?" he says.

"One, two, three," they count off.

"Good, good, good," the man says.

ʒ

The doctor knocks. "Hello?" she says, the way you'd call to your distracted daughter in the next room.

The woman is ready. She's bleeding again. Dripping onto the table, just like last time.

"So?" the doctor asks. "Those little hearts slowing down at all?" Her hair is braided, the braid coiled around her head.

"They felt kind of weird last night. Like something was happening to them."

The doctor is setting up for the ultrasound.

"If the bleeding stops," the woman asks, "Does that mean I'm cured? What will happen to the hearts?" She's still embarrassed to be bleeding onto the table, but now it feels necessary, a small step toward a bigger goal.

"I assume," the doctor says, "If the hearts stop pumping, they will either atrophy and fall out, or get absorbed."

"Absorbed?"

"To be honest, we don't know what we're dealing with. The main thing is to stop the bleeding. How we're going to do that, I don't know yet. A little cold," she says, before pressing the gelled-up probe to the woman's abdomen.

It feels wonderful. "Are they," the woman starts, "Are they okay? I mean, is it bad?"

The doctor gives her a sympathetic glance, then looks at the black and white image on the screen. "Ah, yes, okay, here they are," she says.

"Have they grown?" the woman asks.

"No, thank god. If anything," the doctor says, "they're smaller than they looked transvaginally."

For a second, the woman misunderstands and thinks the doctor is suggesting that her vagina somehow looks transgender, and maybe it's what she did to the hearts that made it look that way.

When she realizes what the doctor meant, the shot of shame passes, but leaves her arms and legs tingly.

"Are they real hearts?" she asks.

The doctor looks confused. She looks at the screen, then back at the woman.

"Maybe I misunderstood," the woman says. "Did you mean that they're actually hearts, real hearts?"

"They're certainly blood-pumpers," the doctor says.

The woman squeezes her thighs together. "You make them sound like monsters."

The doctor hands the woman a towel to wipe the gel from her skin.

"You don't think they're going to develop, do you?"

The doctor smiles. "Into what?"

"More?"

"More hearts? I don't think you have to worry about that."

"But. Why are they just hearts?"

The doctor gives the woman a closed-lip smile. "I don't know the answer to that," she says.

"But. Why do I have these little hearts?"

"I don't know that either. To be honest, why doesn't matter, long as we can fix it."

The woman was premed when she started college, but one year in, her advisor suggested she switch her focus. *You're looking for answers we don't have*, he said.

"How are you going to fix it?" the woman asks.

"Now that's a good question. Why don't you get dressed, and we'll talk in my office."

◌

The woman has never been in the doctor's private office. It's full of plants and smells like popcorn. The doctor is at her desk.

"Have a seat," she tells the woman. Behind her is a window that looks out at the parking lot.

"Don't be nervous," the doctor says. "We're going to take good care of you. First things first. We need to address the blood loss that making you feel so crumby."

The woman clenches her pelvic muscles, as if to give the hearts a grateful squeeze.

"There are two options," the doctor is telling her. "First option is a transfusion."

The woman pictures that: a tube stretched between them, over the desk, one side connected to the woman, the other to the doctor, blood running between them.

That's when she sees the triplets and their dad enter the parking lot with a woman who must be their surrogate. She's dark-skinned, wearing a dress with a sash that wraps around her big belly.

The kids jump into the car: one, two, three, and their dad leans in—buckle, buckle, buckle, then stands and walks to the driver's seat, waving to the surrogate, who walks off on her own.

The doctor is telling the woman about the second option, an experimental medication they would tailor to her specific needs.

The man and the triplets drive off, and the surrogate walks in the opposite direction.

"If I get a transfusion," the woman asks, "wouldn't the hearts pump out the transfused blood?"

"They might not want to pump foreign blood. We don't know. But you'd have more blood regardless."

The woman sees the surrogate sit down at the bus stop across the street. She cradles her belly in her arms.

The truth is that every fetus is at least half-foreign to its mother. It is something that has always bothered the woman, she realizes. It seems gross. And what about women who were impregnated by anonymous sperm donors, or worse, raped into pregnancy.

Bodies, the woman thinks, her body at least, was meant to be singular.

She doesn't want her hearts pumping foreign blood.

∽

The team has to monitor the woman for seven days before she can begin the medication, due to protocol.

Two days in, her roommate comes home and says, "You're never going to believe it." She's smiling but looks like she's been crying, her blue mascara smudged.

For a second the woman thinks her roommate is going to say that she too has hearts in her uterus, and her bleeding is way worse than the woman's. But no. She says that her boyfriend proposed. "And," she says, "I can't believe I didn't start with this—that poem I wrote about you and your hearts?"

"I didn't know you wrote a poem about me."

"It shot out of me, last night, fully formed. I sent it to my agent, and he already found a home for it. At," she says, "You ready? *The New Yorker*. This is a big deal. I mean, marrying the boy is obviously big too, but a poem in *The New Yorker*? It's like we're going to be in *The New Yorker* together. What am I going to do without you?" She frowns hyperbolically.

"What did you say about me and the hearts?"

"I wrote it so fast I barely remember. My agent said it made him cry, though."

"From happiness?"

The roommate shrugs and smiles. Probably, she's already thinking about her next poem. She can turn anything into literary sunshine.

∽

The woman does not get permission from her team to start the experimental medication because she keeps fainting, and her next ultrasound, a week later, shows cuts and scarring that weren't there on the first scan. The hearts are beating faster in response.

She needs to have them removed.

℞

It's raining on the day of the extraction, but inside the hospital, it's warm and dry, the rain a comforting pitter patter.

And the doctor is there, her long hair tucked inside a blue surgical cap that matches the woman's.

Once it's over, the doctor says, she'll be fine.

"But we didn't figure out what it means," the woman says from the operating table.

"We can talk about it later," the doctor says.

"Later? Where? At your house?" The woman pictures that, a kitchen table with a red checkered cloth, a hearth.

"You starting to feel drowsy?" the doctor asks, resting her hand on the woman's shoulder.

Somewhere, a voice says, *Hello? One, two, three?*

The woman blinks. Then the green-eyed triplets appear, hovering over her, six eyes glowing in the bright light. *What's happening to you?* the triplets ask. *You're falling apart.*

The woman feels heat between her legs. Then the hearts appear, floating in the air, reaching for the triplets. *You said you like feeling dizzy. You said you wanted the doctor's attention.*

Tell the hearts to stop, the triplets say. *They're getting blood everywhere. It smells bad. We're trying to sing.*

We're trying to sing too, the hearts say.

Sun shines into the room, but it must be literary sunshine. There are no windows in the operating room.

"Okay," the doctor says. "Count backward from ten."

Come with us, the triplets say. *It's not too late. You want frozen yogurt?*

But then they break apart, arms and legs, eyes and ears, toenails and teeth—all of it floating above her. Then the surrogate is there, trying to gather their parts, like she has to get them back inside her.

"Wait," the woman says. She wants to tell the doctor that she has no one to take her home. "One, two, three?" she says.

As she loses consciousness, she sees a dense forest full of trees, their limbs reaching for the sun, her little hearts twirling in the air, reaching too, showers raining down.

Then she sees her grandfather, his big ears and sweet brown eyes. He's driving a bus, weaving through the trees. *I'm here to take you home*, he says. Her grandfather, who died when she was only six, who took care of her when her mother was at work.

Did you forget about me? he asks, the bus almost toppling as he makes the final turn on the uneven ground.

Then he's in front of her, smiling. She remembers this feeling, the way she felt when he looked at her, amazed, the physical sensation of it, his body, alive, with hers.

He steps off the bus and holds out his arms. *My sunshine,* he says. *Where are you going? Do you see these trees?* He stretches his arms up into the air. *Don't faint,* he says. *There's so much to see.*

Rough in Comparison

FIVE KISSES

On the couch in her parents' living room. The couch is mauve, and it's made of suede. *Poor little calf,* Zoe says, and she pets the couch. *I'm sure your mommy loved you.* She leans her head against the back cushion and kisses it, a gentle kiss, and when she sits up, he says, in a rush, *Can I kiss you?* She pauses, considering. She clears her throat and nods. *Sure, Colin,* she says. *Go for it.* Then they're kissing, his tongue touching hers, touching the roof and sides of her mouth, all that softness—her mouth has got to be abnormally soft. But she's not making any noise—there's no loud breathing, no moans from deep in her throat. She's just poking her tongue at his, like she's trying to push it away, like she's annoyed to find it in her mouth again and again and again. All of this last for less than a minute because he forgets to breathe. Once he remembers, if he were to start breathing, he'd be panting, so he pulls away, which is the right thing to do because he was beginning to hate her. They've been friends for a year at this point. He's in tenth grade, and she's in eleventh grade, and after this kiss, they don't talk for one week.

CR

In the balcony during assembly. They're not supposed to be in the balcony, but they've been there all morning—this was Zoe's idea, to skip their classes, hide between the benches. She brought snacks and a deck of cards. It's November, three months after the couch kiss. The room below is crowded and noisy. Zoe leans toward Colin. *Hey,* she says. He can feel her breath on his neck. It makes his skin tingle; it's not painful, but almost. *We should make out,* she whispers, and he gets the sense it's sort of a joke, sort of a dare, so he says, *Really? Are you serious?* and then she's kissing him. She bites at his lips and tongue, and he doesn't know how to respond—it hurts and feels out of control. Her tongue moves so fast he feels like he's spending the whole time trying to catch it.

CR

In her car, the day before she leaves to spend the summer in Europe. It's late, and they're parked in front of his house. They've spent the whole evening driving, going nowhere, listening to the mix tapes she made for her trip, sad love songs, all of them. He doesn't want Zoe looking at his house, its broken fence, the boarded window, the overgrown lawn. He closes his eyes, as if that will help. Everything is about to change. She's leaving him to get cultured, and when she comes back, she won't be the same, and they won't be the same, whatever they are. For the first time, he's aware of his heart and lungs inside his chest. They feel heavy and swollen. *I'm dying for real this time,* he thinks, so opens his eyes, turns to her and says: *Can I kiss you you can say no.* One sentence. She nods, but he only touches his lips to hers.

CR

In front of the biggest house on her street. It's Thanksgiving, three months into his junior year and her senior year. They meet outside her house at eight in the evening, and she's tipsy on wine, her lips and teeth stained purple. They walk up and down the streets. Expensive cars line the sidewalks. Yellow leaves glow in the streetlights. Some of the houses are close enough to the street that they can see inside. So they stop and stare: these other lives they could be living. *Every house looks more comforting than mine,* she says. And he says, *Every house is more comforting than mine.* It's cold outside, and he give her his jacket—in his head she's his girlfriend, and she loves him, but she's shy. They're both sad, they're both lonely, so they belong together. He forces himself to believe this until he works up the courage and says, *Let's stop walking for a second,* and then: *Let's kiss for a second.* It's been half a year, and she kisses differently now, pressing her whole body against him: a movie kiss, and it's wonderful, the cold air swirling around them, a moment of quiet, of heat, all theirs, like sinking, but good, all good. He hugs her tight, but she pulls back. *I'm sorry,* she says. *It just feels weird. Can we go home? I think I should go home.*

☙

Behind the big rock next to the gymnasium, after Zoe's graduation. This is the rock where kids played kissing games in middle school, but she never played. *What's wrong with me? Why was I so shy and ridiculous?* Her black gown is open; underneath, she's wearing a silky white dress that looks like a slip, that clings. He can see the shape of her, more than he's seen before. *I've missed out on the best years of my life,* she says. *Do you realize that?* She kicks at the rock, looks up at him. He feels it in the center of his chest, that look, almost like she's pinching him there. Then she kisses him, long kisses this time, her hands on his face, and his arms hanging at his sides. He can't touch her; he can't take that chance. He spends the whole time wondering when it's going to stop, and then it does.

CR

ONE MORE KISS?

Colin sat in the waiting room and pictured Zoe in the dentist's chair, her head thrown back and her mouth wide open. It was August, one week before Zoe had to leave for college.

Colin was supposed to be at work, a paid internship at a chemical engineering firm. His high school counselor told him that success at this internship would basically guarantee a scholarship to MIT the following year. But Zoe had a dentist appointment, and she wanted Colin to take her.

The waiting room was gray, black, and burgundy, sophisticated and sanitized with glass tables on Oriental rugs. Instead of folding chairs, they had leather couches. Instead of magazines, there were art books. Instead of radio music, they played Mozart.

Colin's T-shirt felt wet and cold under his arms. His hair felt itchy against his head and neck. He was sure that the man sitting across from him, who was wearing a perfectly tailored and wrinkle-free suit, who seemed to be part of the décor, could tell that Colin's head was itchy, his armpits wet.

Colin imagined himself as a sweatless dentist. Girls like Zoe would walk into his office, lie back and open their mouths. He pictured himself lying on top of Zoe in the chair, her mouth open and his hands inside, scraping her teeth with his fingernails. He'd rub against her; they'd grope in the locked, sanitized room.

The man in the gray suit, on top of everything else, had hair as silky and straight as a rabbit's fur, but thick too. Colin's father had hair like that, but he was balding now and didn't have a suit that fit him. These days, often, he wore pajamas bottoms when he drove his cab. Colin had his mother's hair, super-tight curls as rough as rope in chaos around his head. He had her complexion too, pale and ruddy, so that any anger or embarrassment announced itself in the flush of their cheeks. At least his face wasn't as fat as his mother's.

Colin stared at the man in the gray suit. He wanted to tell him that he got a perfect score on his math SAT, that he'd be going to MIT, that wanting silky straight hair was nothing but racism. But the man in the gray suit was just sitting there flipping through an art book. Did men like that really care about art? Colin had no right to judge, really. He didn't know anything about art either, nothing that Zoe hadn't told him, at least. He didn't understand it, not the way she did.

You're not supposed to understand it, he imagined her saying response. *You're just supposed to feel what you feel. Experience it.* What he felt was fury, at this man, for existing, provoking his anger.

Two years, five kisses—he ran these figures through his head every day, but still couldn't make sense of them.

And that thought—Zoe—like the sudden fear of a test you had somehow forgotten, reminded him of the dentist with his fingers inside her mouth.

Colin could never be a dentist. He saw that now. He would hurt people, people like this man. He wouldn't be able to stop himself.

CR

Zoe arrived at the reception desk with a blue folder containing the entire history of her teeth. She stood with her elbows resting on the counter.

She was an optical illusion: his eyes wide open, she was a rich girl, just slightly rebellious with her purple hair and raggedy red corduroys cut into shorts. She knew how to talk to the receptionist about insurance; she was confident and oblivious in a way that only rich people can be. But when he squinted his eyes, she was scared and insecure, as out of place and uncomfortable as he was. He wanted to walk over there, put his hands on her hips and turn her body to face him. Right in front of the receptionist, he'd lick her teeth to see if the dentist had done a good job.

Finally, she was walking toward him, but she didn't say anything.

She just sat down, next to Colin, eyes on her lap as if they were strangers. Then she leaned toward him and whispered in his ear. "You waiting for someone?" she asked. "You looking for a date?"

Colin raised his head in just enough time to see that the man in the gray suit was staring at them. Colin felt stuck in that moment, as if the sweat from his body had glued him to the chair. The man flashed a smile, not friendly: a quick reprimand.

But Zoe grabbed hold of Colin's wrist, pulled him up and led him to the exit. Then that man was in their past. He didn't matter.

CR

In the car, Zoe pushed her feet against the dashboard of his mother's dirty, beat up, dark brown Dodge. She chain-smoked cigarettes out the window.

When they entered her neighborhood, the grass turned cartoon green, and the trees formed a canopy of shade over the streets. Behind them, Colin imagined a street-cleaner sweeping Zoe's cigarette ash and butts, disinfecting the air which his mother's car couldn't help but pollute.

It was too much to think about: the complicated world-wide class system, those who dirty the earth, those who clean it, and those who pay to have it cleaned. What he wanted was anarchy, survival of the least fit, the most enraged. No weapons or money, just bodies verses bodies. Even language he could do without. He could reach over and touch her, kiss any part of her. She wouldn't think about it, and he wouldn't think about it, they'd just feel it: the sensation of skin sliding against skin.

"Do you think you'll have sex in college?" he asked her.

"Definitely," she said, "But only with lab animals, rats mostly."

"I'm serious. It's gotta be easier in college, for girls at least."

"Probably not for me," she said. Guys weren't into her, that's what she always said—as if Colin didn't count.

He pictured her at college, far away, artistic boys spreading her legs and knowing things he didn't know: the exact color of her nipples, the way she'd move her hips, what she'd say afterward.

"We should have sex before you leave," he decided to say. "Just to get the first time over with."

"I hate the way you think about these things," she said.

"I don't," he said. "I don't think about it that way. I don't. I don't even think about it, okay?"

He could feel her looking at him, but he kept his eyes on the road. He pictured his senior year. He'd see everything he was seeing right then: he could drive through her neighborhood, dip fries in cheese at the diner she liked, ask to hold the bunnies at the pet store at the mall. He'd be at home, and yet, somehow, he'd feel homesick. He felt it already, this ache in his chest that made it hard to breathe.

Zoe dropped her cigarette into the street and rolled up the window, then rolled it right back down. She always forgot there was no air conditioning.

"This car is disgusting," he said. "I don't know why you won't drive your car. And I never want to have sex, okay? Never. Not with anyone. I just want air-conditioning."

Zoe lit another cigarette. "You're funny," she said.

"You too," he said. He paused at the stop sign and looked at her. "And beautiful," he said. "You're beautiful."

Zoe didn't say anything in response. Colin felt the compliment hanging in the air, echoing again and again, filling the car like heat: *You're beautiful. Oh, you're so fucking beautiful. Did I mention that I think you're beautiful? Because I think you're beautiful.*

The humidity and cigarette smoke were making him sick to his stomach. He tried to swallow, but there was a lump in his throat, like children get when they're holding back tears. He was sure that adults were not supposed to feel this way.

At the next stoplight, he turned to her. She had her chin to her chest, purple strands of hair hanging in her face. She was concentrating on her cigarette, staring at it as if she didn't know how it got in her hand, as if this cigarette were mysterious, the most interesting thing in the car.

Then he watched her touch the orange, lit end to her leg and quickly pull it away. "What? Wait, what are you doing?" he said. Again she pushed the cigarette to her leg, holding it there a little bit longer this time. He could smell hair burning.

"Stop it," he said. He sounded angry. He was a hateful parent who didn't want to understand. "Stop it," he said again. "Please, Zoe, please just stop." *I love you*, he wanted to say, but he knew it would only make things worse.

"It doesn't hurt," she said. "It feels good."

"Then burn my leg," he told her. "If you have to burn something, burn me."

"Light's green," she said.

It was as if she had built a barrier between them—somehow, without warning, turned into a stranger. A person stronger than he was, more daring and distant.

But he could detach himself too. He could let her think about whatever she was thinking about, without needing to know what it was. He kept his eyes on the road. He drove two more blocks. "Why'd you burn your leg?" he asked.

"No reason," she said.

"But what were you thinking about?"

"Nothing," she said. "I wasn't thinking about anything."

"So you thoughtlessly burnt your leg? Nothing's bothering you?"

"Okay," she said "Fine." He heard her inhale, the squeak of her seat as she repositioned herself and dropped her feet to the floor. "I was thinking about Mr. Ruskin," she said.

Colin felt his brain swell in his skull. Mr. Ruskin was their high school's art teacher, and Zoe had been obsessed with him since Colin met her. He was the only teacher who wore jeans and smoked cigarettes. He had a following of shy and awkward girls and boys at the school. Colin thought Zoe's crush was embarrassing. Everyone liked Mr. Ruskin. The choice was too obvious.

"Why would thinking about Mr. Ruskin make you burn your leg?" he asked.

He looked at her now. She stared back, but didn't say anything.

"What?" he said. "You miss him or something? You wish you didn't have to go to college so you could stay here with him? You probably wish you were with him right now, don't you? You can be honest, Zoe. I'd understand."

"Forget it," she said. "I'm not having this conversation." She put her feet back on the dashboard.

"I'm sorry," he told her. "I'm sorry. I didn't mean to say it like that."

"I know," she said. "It's fine."

She hung her arm out the window and looked outside for the rest of the ride.

ജ

Twenty minutes later, they were sitting on a bench swing in her backyard. Colin loved the red slates that lined the roof of the Prizer's house, topping it like a beautiful warrior cap. The exterior walls were painted in such a bright white they seemed purposely designed to attract vandals and thieves. Strange that Colin knew their alarm code.

He'd have a house like this if he could, a fortress. He'd never leave.

Zoe finished her cigarette and buried it in a planter next to the bench. There must have been cigarettes twisted in the roots of every plant in the yard, scattered throughout the soil and garden. But no one seemed to notice. Zoe's parents were never at home, at least not when Colin was around. They worked all the time, he realized— that's why Colin got to go to private school, because people like the Prizers worked hard at respectable jobs and paid so much for their children's education that it was enough to support the poor kids too. It made Colin feel like a stray dog, part of the family in some way.

Zoe had her knees pulled to her chest now. He felt like he'd sat down next to her uninvited. The backyard, its gardens and trees and cobbled brick path, looked like a movie set. The two of them on the bench were characters he didn't understand.

He didn't care if she was quiet, though. He didn't care as long as he could sit there and witness it, whatever she decided to do. He didn't care if they sat there all day without saying a word. He just wanted her there next to him—sitting with him, him of all people.

"Do you want to see what I learned yesterday?" She stood up from the bench and walked onto the grass. "Ready?"

It was the first thing she'd said since they got to her house. He thought she might do a strip dance or recite a poem, or just as easily, set her hair on fire.

Instead, she raised her arms in the air and did a slow, awkward cartwheel. He saw her stomach for just a second, her hair on the grass, her thighs. She landed on her butt and laughed. Her hair was in her face and her clothes were twisted around her body, and she was a girl playing in the grass, performing just for him.

He wanted to have sex with her. He wanted to be at his house with her, where everything was small and unintimidating, where she wouldn't be a rich girl, but just a girl. He wanted to have sex with her in his bed, and he wanted her to bleed onto his blanket and sheets. He'd let her blood soak into the fabric and stain it, then he could have that, at least.

"Colin," she said, "I have something to tell you."

"You're going to the Olympics?"

"No, Colin, I'm serious. You're not going to like this."

She was picking at her cuticles, staring down at her fingers. She wasn't even looking at him.

But she did this all the time. She'd say, *I have something to tell you*, and then she'd say she might be in love with her sister, or she was thinking of moving to Iceland.

"Then, what?" he asked.

Zoe bit her upper lip. He could see her bottom teeth. "I've been having an affair with Andrew Ruskin for about a year," she said. "But it's over now."

She didn't smile. She wasn't joking. Andrew Ruskin. She called him Andrew. Andy. Zoe's Lover. Child-Fucker. Her Secret Lover— the very best kind there is.

It felt like gravity got stronger all of a sudden, like he couldn't possibly move. So he sat there and tried to imagine it: Zoe, who does cartwheels in the grass, who's kissed him but that's it, who told Colin he's the smartest person she knows, who said she loves him, like a brother, but still. Who has been having an affair with her teacher.

"Say something," she said. But she was twenty feet away from him, and the space between them felt enormous. The universe, actually, felt enormous, unrecognizable. This was the first time Colin was seeing anything.

Zoe had moved onto the grass and done that cartwheel just so she could unburden herself. This was the reason she wanted to spend the day with him.

"Please," she said now. "Please say something?"

But he didn't know what to say. He wanted to say that he hated her, because he did, he hated her. But he had no right to be angry, he knew that, and it only made him angrier.

"What am I supposed to say?" he asked. He actually wanted an answer. But all she did was look at him and smile, like this was the most pity she'd ever felt for anyone.

"It's your life," he said. "I don't have anything to say."

He watched Zoe lift her hair in her hands and twist it into a bun. He watched the purple strands spin around her head again and again. There was her face. All that year he had been looking at it, and still he didn't know.

He always loved to watch her play with her hair, pull it back. All of her features looked so defined once her hair was out of her face. But now her face looked different, older, used.

Mr. Ruskin's hands had been on her face, in her hair.

She stood up and brushed dirt and grass from her clothes. He still loved her. He couldn't stop himself. But he didn't know her, not at all apparently, so what he felt was anger, for everything that made her the least bit attractive.

When she started walked toward him, he felt like he was having an asthma attack, his airways swelling, yet Zoe was perfectly fine. The fact that the space between them was shrinking had no effect on her.

When she sat down, the bench rocked slowly back and forth. Colin tried desperately to hold it still with his feet. Her corduroys were touching his leg, and she put her hand on his back. She might as well have said, *This isn't about you. I'm pretending that I feel bad for you only to make it completely obvious that this is not about you.*

Her hand on his back, and her hand had been on Mr. Ruskin's back, his naked back. And that's what this was about—Zoe and Mr. Ruskin.

Colin was supposed to be at his internship right then. He didn't even call to say he wasn't coming, and now they'd probably fire him. He'd lose everything because of Zoe, because of Mr. Ruskin.

"Are you okay?" she asked. "Say something. Do you want to ask me anything? What do you want to know?"

He wanted to know everything. He wanted to know why his dad was a taxi driver and hers was a doctor, why everyone thought Colin was so smart when really, obviously, he was an idiot. And most of all, he wanted to know every detail of the sex they'd had, every kiss, every loving word. He wanted her to make lists, draw graphs, track everything she ever felt. He wanted her to count the number of times she wished he were Mr. Ruskin.

"Why did you tell me?" he asked.

"Because his wife found out, and she left him, and he told me he's lost everything he's ever loved and we can never speak again."

A few strands of her hair were falling against her face. Her cheeks looked red against the purple strands. He knew he was sup-posed to feel sorry for her. That must have been her intension. And maybe she thought he would be relieved, because it was over. But he didn't want it to be over and he didn't want to feel sorry for her; he only wanted to feel bad for himself. He wanted her to say that, in losing Andrew Ruskin, she too lost everything she'd ever loved. If Zoe would just tell Colin to go away, that she didn't need him, didn't want him and never had—then he'd feel satisfied. He just wanted to know for sure that she was using him, that she was only doing this because he was all she had left.

CR

An hour later, they're sitting on Zoe's bed, and Colin feels nostalgic. He feels like he's visiting the room of someone who has died. Under her desk is a shrine to Tori Amos, CDs and candles surrounding a mounted poster of Amos at the piano, looking blissful, red hair bright and everything else muted. The shrine is sort of joke, but not really. Now, to Colin, it's funny and sad at the same time. Zoe's right there, but he's thinking about all of this like it's a memory: Zoe and her shrine to Tori Amos. He imagines telling someone about it like it was something he never managed to appreciate about her.

"If you had to choose between Mr. Ruskin and Tori Amos," he asks, "who would you choose?"

"Tori," she says. "Definitely." Colin's happy to hear this until he realizes it just means he's knocked down a notch. Tori Amos, Mr. Ruskin, Colin. Maybe. If he's lucky.

He wants her to rank everyone in her life. If you were stuck on a desert island, if there was a flood and you had a raft and room for only one other person, if Mr. Ruskin and I were inside a burning building, if we were both dying and needed your extra kidney, if I were the last man on earth.

"I wish I were a girl," he tells her. "I wish we were girlfriends. Not gay ones—I didn't mean it like that."

"I'm leaving in a week," she says.

I'll be dead by then, he thinks.

Zoe is touching the burn on her leg. She'll still have that burn when she's sitting on the bed in her new dorm room. Colin pictures it, Zoe sitting on a small bed, all alone, no friends, broken hearted. He wants to go with her. They could start over, away from her home and his home, Mr. Ruskin, everything that's already happened.

He might never sit on her bed again, he realizes.

He wants to comfort her, give her a hug, tell her it's going to be okay, all of it. And he wants to tell her not to go, to stay with him, even if all they do is sit together and feel miserable.

But can't comfort her because he'd feel too stupid. He'd feel like a pushover. All he can think about is her graduation, the way Mr. Ruskin gave her a hug and held on a bit too long. And Colin didn't even care, he watched and didn't care, because he thought he and Zoe were the ones with a secret that day, their kiss on the playground. Their kiss—kisses, actually—which were a joke, apparently, which meant nothing.

"Are you in love with him?" Colin asks.

"You really want to know?"

"Yes," he says. "I mean, no. It doesn't matter."

"I feel better, though," she says. The look she gives him, it's like she's in love with him, like she's seeing him for the first time, how wonderful he is. But it's too late; this feels even worse.

"I'm glad you're here," she says, "and that I told you and everything."

"Just stop," he says. "I haven't done anything. I barely said a thing."

"I know," she says. She looks down at her leg and touches the burn again. This time she looks happy. She looks smug. He wishes he had a burning cigarette, that he could make a burn on his own leg that's worse than hers. Or he'd press the fire to her face, he'd hurt her, just like Mr. Ruskin did. The scar would last forever.

"Do you want some tea?" she asks. "You look really uncomfortable. I can make you some tea."

It's as if she's given him a horrible disease, but now that he's sick, she's all better.

"I'll have some tea," he tells her. "You can make me tea if you want to." He'll take the tea, and he'll have to pour it onto his legs. He can't let her take care of him—not now, not after she shut him out for so long.

She leans toward him and wraps her arms around his shoulders. It's the worst feeling he's ever experienced. It feels like her body is covered in pins and they're pricking his skin.

But he's also getting hard.

He needs it to stop, to stop feeling like he wants her. He feels the pins and needles everywhere, under her hands, spreading down his back. So he starts pushing himself against her. He wraps his legs around her hips, and he pushes himself against her like it's a confession, time for his confession now.

She's telling him to stop, but she isn't pulling away.

He's pushing harder now, and she's breathing harder—finally

she's breathing as hard as he is. It turns him on even more. But he's not just thinking about Zoe. He's thinking about his disgusting parents and their disgusting house, this big pristine home he's in, the scholarship to MIT, which he doesn't even want anymore. He's still pushing against her, and it feels like everything he's ever wanted and everything he's ever hated all at the same time. He's grasping her now, pulling her closer.

He won't let himself stop. He keeps going until, finally, he really has ruined everything.

Now We're Photogenic

Chase and Sarah are searching for a headache cure. They're walking down Sixth Avenue and stopping in any store that might offer relief. They've been doing this for hours now, ever since Sarah told Chase that she had a headache and Chase realized that his head hurt too.

Of course, Chase almost always has a headache, a constant dull pounding that flares up at the slightest suggestion of someone else's suffering. A commercial for headache medicine featuring the afflicted can leave him tormented for hours.

When he was a boy, Chase watched his maternal grandmother die of brain cancer. Now, as he and Sarah make their way through the mattress department of Macy's, Chase imagines a lump of cells the size of a small potato sprouting in his head, army-green vines snaking their way through the grooves in his brain, penetrating the soft tissue and borrowing bullet-like holes from one side to the other. He worries that the sprouts will weave their way out, reaching for light, out through his ears, his eye sockets, his nostrils.

Before they left the apartment, Chase and Sarah had tried aspirin and ibuprofen, sinus and allergy medication, which they sprayed up their noses, caffeine, sex, nicotine, and finally Gatorade, to counteract their former failed attempts. Now they pretend they're shopping for a mattress—they rest on their backs in the air-conditioned store. It could be the heat, the persistent summer sun and humidity; it could be exhaustion.

"How would you characterize your pain?" Chase asks Sarah. "What color?" he asks. "If you had to describe it as a color." Chase keeps a diary of his headaches, documents not only the location of the pain but its likeness to particular colors, smells, and sounds. He takes note of any memories provoked by the headache, any associated mood-states. It always helps him, and now he wants to help Sarah.

"Do you see any color at all?" Chase asks.

"Blue," Sarah says finally. She's staring at the ceiling, and Chase has to prop himself up to look at her.

"Are you sure?" he asks her. He's leaning over her now, his head right above hers. "What shade of blue?" he asks.

"Midnight blue," she says quickly, as if she hasn't given it a moment's thought. The plastic on the mattress makes a slight suction noise as she rolls over to face the wall.

"Are you sure?" he asks. "Midnight blue? It's just that blue is sort of a comforting color, don't you think? Are you sure it's not more of a purple? Or turquoise blue! Did you mean turquoise?"

"Forget it, Chase," she says. "Please, forget it."

In his diary, Chase will frequently sketch the overall landscape of his pain. Sometimes his work is metaphoric—he'll draw a bird's nest holding a hard-boiled egg that's been coiled in barbed wire, for example; other times he'll try to draw a realistic portrait of his brain under the headache's influence, the way it would appear if his brain were somehow projected from his skull onto a blank screen. In these moments, the headache acts as his muse, describing his brain to him in lush and sickening detail.

"We should close our eyes," he says to Sarah. "It could be the bright light—all that sun and now these fluorescent bulbs—they're both carcinogens, you know."

Sarah doesn't respond, and now that Chase has his eyes closed, he feels like he's all alone in that bed, a crazy man who's mistaken a department store for his own bedroom. The headaches could have brought them closer together, but he's ruined it. And his headache is sharpening—it's crimson and lime green and the two colors are clashing inside his head, endless blaring zigzags of blinding, flashing color. He can already feel the sprouts poking and beginning to curl tightly around the back of his eyeballs.

଼

Sarah leads Chase from the mattress department to women's dresses, where he begins to search for the exact color of his headache in the myriad fabrics. He spots a sweater with golden circles on its sleeves— he can feel those exact circles colliding with force right behind his eyes, his entire frontal cortex lassoed by the resulting vibrations. Then he finds a long skirt covered in small coral flowers with olive stems; armed with sharp thorns, he can feel those flowers staggering like an army of drunks along the grooved surface of his brain.

"You know my grandmother died of a brain tumor," he tells Sarah.

"You know what," she says, "My headache is completely gone. Maybe if you stop thinking about it yours would go away too." She's working her way through racks and racks of dresses, Chase following behind.

When he grabs onto her pocketbook to balance himself—he's starting to feel a bit faint—Sarah lifts a sundress from the rack. "Do you like this?" she asks him. The dress is light blue with small yellow flowers. "You said blue is comforting, right?"

The walls in the dress department are painted a pale but aggressive shade of purple; the music piped through the sound-system is classical but chaotic; there is a flute solo that features long shrill notes.

"You know what your problem is," Sarah is telling him, "there's nothing else for you to focus on. Nothing is enough to distract you." She has at least four sizes of that blue dress hanging over her forearm. "Nothing is enough to distract you, so you focus on your head all day long and of course with all that focusing you're bound to discover some slight discomfort in there. Now wait a second," she says. "Just stay here."

Sarah walks into the dressing area for only a second; then she's back and she takes Chase by the wrist. "You're coming with me," she says. She pulls him into a stall at the far side of the empty dressing room, and this is how it starts. "Don't worry," she says, locking them inside. "I won't be taking off my clothes. I know that wouldn't help you."

ʘ

Twenty minutes later, Chase is sitting on an elevated stool in front of a makeup counter. He's wearing the sundress and he's watching Sarah smear different shades of lipstick onto the back of his hand. She presses hard, leaving clumps.

As the saleswoman approaches, he can hear her heels click-clacking behind the counter. She stops in front of them and looks Chase up and down, but she doesn't say anything. When she walks away, she seems almost sad.

Chase holds himself still, allowing Sarah to rub lipstick onto his lips. He's thinking about his grandmother again, but not her tumor this time, her pocketbook—her enormous pocketbook—which smelled, he now realizes, exactly like lipstick.

When he closes his eyes so that Sarah can apply shadow, he imagines that he inhabits his grandmother's body—he's a skinny, wrinkled old woman who's too sick and weak to put on his own makeup.

Will you marry me? his grandmother had asked him two days before she died. *I've been in love with you for years*, she told him. She had reached out for his hand, but Chase, eleven years old at the time, would not let his dying grandmother touch him. *Until death do we part*, she had said.

When Chase opens his eyes, Sarah is grinning. "Are you feeling self-conscious?" she asks him. "Are you thinking about it? Are you really giving it some thought?" She looks at him seriously now. "Everyone's staring at you, Chase. All these people," she says. "They think you're a freak. Most of them despise you. They fear for their children when they look at you. They want to kill you, Chase, and you know what? They'd kill you faster than a brain tumor ever could. Now close your eyes," she tells him. "I'm not done yet."

He follows her orders; he sits still; he closes his eyes. And he loves the feeling of it. He loves that he's wearing a dress, that she bought it for him and he's wearing it and now she's taking care of him. He knows he should probably be frightened, or he should worry about their relationship. At very least he should feel embarrassed, but he doesn't. On the contrary, actually: he feels at peace; he feels protected.

His eyes are still closed, and he listens to the sound of voices and footsteps getting louder as they approach him and then slowly dissipating once they've passed him by. He starts to hear all of these sounds like they're part of a song sung in round, the unique sound of a particular couple or small group as they become audible, then their slow crescendo, then quieter and quieter until they're inaudible, one set after the next making its own contribution to the layers of sound. And behind them there is still that classical music, but it's changed—there's a cello now and an instrument Chase can't identify except to say that it is similar to a French horn, yet much more elegant.

Meanwhile, Sarah's fingers are on his face, tilting his head this way and that. He hears her breathing—it's the sound closest to him—and as he listens, he feels more in love with her than he ever has before. And his headache, miraculously, is blue—it's the color of his dress. He imagines that the fabric is inside his brain, smothering the sprouts and blanketing the tumor.

16 Days of Glory

After our parents left for Vermont, Ruby and I spent most of our time waiting for the Olympics. *The world is coming to Los Angeles!* the commercials told us, and the announcer's tone was so excited and serious it seemed to imply that every American should prepare.

That summer was going to be a turning point for our family. We were in the final stages of a move to rural Vermont, where my parents were rebuilding a house they planned to have ready by the start of the school year. Once the house was inhabitable, even barely so, we'd all move in and complete the finishing touches as a family. We'd already chosen the stencils we'd use on the walls in each of our bedrooms. Mine was going to be silver, turquoise, and black.

In the meantime, my job—mine and Ruby's—was to have the fun summer that my mother said we'd earned. We could contribute to the house by holding down our current fort, a converted garage in the Philadelphia suburbs. The beauty of the garage apartment was that it looked like a mini-version of the other houses in the neighborhood. My mother liked to point out that you could look at a picture of the garage and a picture of a real house, and you couldn't necessarily tell which one was which.

But Philadelphia's Main Line was only a stepping-stone in our journey. The goal was to educate ourselves in multiple ways, and the four years of high-class learning we'd done in the suburbs—in one of the best school districts in the country—was coming to an end. It was time for us to learn from the land, to shed our un-scuffed shoes and make ourselves interesting.

My mother was the architect of our journey. People in my life have often argued that the choices she made on behalf of our family were unsettling or even unhinged, and I can't fully deny that. All I can say is that her conviction and spunk were so impressive to me that I find it hard, even now, to fault her for anything she's done or failed to do. The parts of myself I treasure the most I inherited from my mother. At my best, I can feel those segments of my DNA light up and sparkle.

ଜ

The morning of the Opening Ceremony, Ruby and I painted our nails with red, white, and blue polish. We rearranged the living room to make space for the beanbags we pulled from our bedroom and placed in front of the television. We hung blankets over the windows and turned on only the twinkle lights that zig-zagged across our living room ceiling, our own stars and sky inside with us. It felt like we were in the stands that way, our beanbags pulled curbside.

Seconds into the ceremony, the cameras panned the stadium, and before we could absorb the grandeur of the crowd and the perfectly placed members of the marching band, we heard a rocket blastoff and saw a man, strapped to a jetpack, launch himself from the stands up into the sky and land at the center of the stadium.

There, on TVs across the globe, was proof that ours was the greatest country in the world. The grass in our stadiums was greener, the energy in our oxygen was greater, and Ruby and I were part of it because we were American and gilded at our core.

I had just turned fifteen, and for the first time in my life, I was an optimist and a patriot. I felt in my bones what my mother had always said: I could create any life I wanted for myself if I was just willing to grab it.

Carl Lewis, Edwin Moses, even Ronald Reagan—they started with the same raw materials I had: a brain and a body and an iron-clad American will to win. For the time being, I had no choice but to dedicate myself to what I could only call *greatness*.

There was speed mounting in me already. I felt like I could run through our neighborhood and emerge somewhere else entirely. What I had in mind wasn't a specific place, but a vast expanse of blue and green with shining spots of gold, a massive canopy of twinkle lights. Beyond the manicured hedges and mansion rooftops that lined our neighborhood, I could forge a magnificent life for myself. My own body was the vehicle to get me there.

ᘓ

The next morning, I began training.

I knew that physical activities requiring skill were not my forte. I didn't have great balance or coordination, but I'd discovered that I could outrun most of my peers, as long as the distance of the run was great enough to bewilder the typical adolescent, most of whom were interested in quick success rather than hard-earned triumph. I enjoyed the sting in my limbs and the weight in my chest that came with prolonged effort. That pain was proof of my fortitude—my delight in it was my greatest asset and the core competency Ruby and I would tap in my training.

I stood in the middle of our living room, held out my arms and swung them around me, a quick succession of almost violent self-hugs. Then I raised my hands above my head, lifted one leg at a time and touched my toes with my fingertips. I learned these moves from the Jane Fonda workout my mother had on video. Ruby must have recognized the specific workout I was doing because she started to hum the song that played in that video. It was terrible to realize she knew that song well enough to sing it.

At the time, I hated Jane Fonda. I hated her ridiculous leg warmers, her hoity-toity lifestyle, and that fluffy, flaxen hair of hers. But more than that, I hated myself for hating her. My mother moved us to the Main Line so we wouldn't be fazed by highbrows like Jane Fonda, but I was fazed. Every time she'd say, *Push it! You can do it!*, I felt worthless. Her particular mix of strength and girliness sickened me. I wanted to strip her of her pink leotard and strangle her with it.

But those first moves I did on the first official day of the 1984 Olympics came straight from her video, and the anger I felt for Jane Fonda was part of what fueled me that summer. I wanted to dig my knuckles into my chest, wrap my fist around that feeling and squash it.

I did the rest of my training that day in front of the television.

What was I training for? We didn't know, and it didn't matter. The only thing I knew was that I was determined to build a life for myself with my newfound desire to win.

I cycled with the cyclists—lying on my back, hips propped, legs pedaling the air. During the women's swimming medley, I lay with my stomach on our small coffee table, perfecting my strokes. My father built that table from scraps he collected at his first demolition job on the Main Line. I pictured myself pulling his energy from that table and funneling it back to my parents in Vermont.

Unfortunately, the more ridiculous I felt trying to move my body the way the Olympians moved theirs, the more difficult it became to do so. I felt my hands and feet getting heavier and heavier until I was panting, my limbs hanging from the sides of the table like the tentacles of a swollen, dead octopus, my torso a bloated blob on the table.

Ruby saw me this way and suggested I take a break, like it was her idea rather than my own failure to endure. "I'll do more tomorrow," I told her. Then I admitted that I didn't actually think I would. "I'm tired," I said. "I might be tired for the rest of my life."

"Stand up," Ruby said then, like she knew exactly how to fix me and getting off that table was the first step.

I was born eleven months before Ruby—for a time that meant I knew a lot more than she did, but we were getting to an age where eleven months didn't mean much in terms of wisdom or even knowledge.

She grabbed my shoulders. He cheeks looked tan and chubby. "Repeat after me," she said: "My hustle and heart set me apart."

I repeated her.

"I win with my will, not with my skill," she said, almost chanting. "I'm gonna kick it where it counts."

I repeated each one, but she ran out of slogans after that, so she said, "To the floor!" and told me to do eleven pushups. She knew that was the most I could do without stopping to rest.

When I finished and stood up in front of her, I felt taller and more powerful.

"Rosie," she said, "Your only job for today is to rest for tomorrow." I could see M&Ms smashed into the grooves of her bottom teeth, tiny pools of brown speckled with bits of yellow, red, and green, and it struck me how deeply I loved her.

For the remainder of that day and through the evening, Ruby and I lay on our beanbags eating M&Ms and Ritz crackers with spray cheese.

"You realize we could be doing anything," Ruby said at one point, and I think we both got the same feeling, that we wanted to do something bigger, but not yet. I was pretty sure that's what she was feeling too because after she said it we both settled deeper into our beanbags.

Every night since our parents left we'd slept in their bed, but that night we camped in the living room, the TV broadcasting long after we'd fallen asleep, the voices of the announcers infiltrating our dreams and beginning to narrate them, the roar of the crowd waking us periodically and filling the whole apartment with the spirit of the games.

CR

The next morning, we took my training outside. Ruby stood at the bottom of the driveway with a clipboard and stopwatch, and I ran around the block as fast as I could.

A powerful beat pulsed inside me, a rhythm that belonged to no song in particular, but to my brain and my body—the rhythm of me at my best. But I was sluggish at first. My skin was buzzing with that groove, but I couldn't get the rest of me in sync.

Ruby suggested I set a goal for myself. "If you say it aloud," she explained, "you're like sixty times more likely to achieve it."

That morning my mother had called to say their plumbing problem was worse than they thought. My father had taken on handyman work in the area, partially to pay for a professional plumber, and partially because people had seen the work he'd done on our house and, according to my mother, were so impressed they insisted on hiring him, but regardless, it had slowed things down considerably. The upside, she said, was that it gave her more time to choose tiles for the bathroom. She promised we were still on track to move in September, but Ruby and I would probably miss the first week of school.

I didn't tell Ruby about the plumbing problem, and I didn't tell my mother that our landlord had called five times looking for her. I didn't want her to send money for rent that she could be spending on the new house. Mr. Federman didn't need our money. He owned tons of properties, all more expensive than ours. It wouldn't make a difference to him if we paid every penny we owed. My mother knew this better than anyone, but I worried she'd think I was too meek to handle the situation myself.

"What's your goal?" Ruby asked me.

"I'm going to run harder and faster," I said. I wanted a goal I could definitely achieve.

I pictured Carl Lewis and Edwin Moses, the thick muscles in their thighs and the beautiful darkness of their skin. I felt each stride I took stripping Ruby's future of pink leotards and girly aerobics routines. I pictured my family outside of our new house in Vermont: strong, proud, and American.

When I turned the corner of my final lap, Ruby was there

jumping and cheering. "That was way faster!" she said, and I chose to believe her.

"I will now run a mile in less than seven minutes," I announced.

There must have been people on the street as I ran, but I didn't see anyone. I could feel the folds of my brain wrap around the muscle in my calves and propel me. I was pumping my own heart, inflating my lungs with my thoughts, generating my own electric speed.

To cover one mile, I had to run a loop four by three blocks long. I did it in six minutes and fifty-eight seconds. It was the first specific goal I'd set and achieved, and it was thrilling.

ℭ

That afternoon we got our weekly care package from our mother. She'd send coupons for free pints of Ben & Jerry's ice cream, treats made from real Vermont maple syrup, and thirty dollars for food and supplies. She also sent Polaroids of the house in every package: a brick wall my father had reconstructed and she had painted, a series of mismatched but coordinated tiles she planned to use in the kitchen, the corner of a room that was going to be Ruby's, where she could fit a drum set and play as loud as she liked. Sometimes we'd find a picture of our dad in the package, making a funny face at the camera. Every box was plastered with stickers advertising Vermont, most of them chosen by our father and featuring a cartoon bear or moose. There was something comforting about the infantile nature of those packages.

It was hot and humid as we walked to Wawa that afternoon. The trees on either side of the street drooped over us, as if weighted by the heat. We could smell freshly cut grass and smoking barbecue coals. As we walked, we ran our fingertips along the dense, carefully shorn bushes that separated the front lawn of each house from the sidewalk.

I liked our neighborhood best in July and August, when most of the kids were away at camp or touring Europe. I was able to appreciate the architecture when I didn't have to worry about bumping into anyone from school. I did have friends there; I just didn't have any friends I wanted to see or talk to.

The diversity of houses in the neighborhood was what my family enjoyed most. We treated the collection like a catalogue of possibilities for our own home. Ruby and I pointed to features we liked and disliked. It was something we always did with our mother—doing it without her made us feel both closer to her and farther away.

Halfway to Wawa, Ruby and I pulled off our T-shirts and walked the streets in just our bikini tops and cutoffs. We were garage-dwellers, soon-to-be daring rural Vermontians—we didn't care what anyone thought, and the breeze on our stomachs felt like its own victory.

I let Ruby convince me to go into the store shirtless. "It's part of your training," she said. "You have to bare yourself. Show Wawa what you're made of." We were molding our new Vermont-selves, and the freedom we felt was thrilling. No one on the Main Line mattered anymore because we no longer had to appeal to them.

I met Gabriel for the first time standing in front of the ice cream cooler that day. He was wearing a Blondie T-shirt and pushing a stroller. He walked over with a smile on his face like he was happy to see us.

"You're the runner!" he said to me. Then he held out his hand. I figured he'd seen me training and I'd impressed him. I gripped his hand tightly, and he squeezed mine back in response, nodding and smiling, like it was the strength he'd expected from me.

Then he moved his eyes to Ruby, and his smile changed slightly. He looked almost amused. "Hello, Ruby," he said, and it was like he'd said, *hold 'em up*, or *you're under arrest*—that's the effect it had on me, the fact that he knew my sister's name.

"Hi there," Ruby said. She crossed her forearms at her stomach and lifted her fingers up and down in a tiny wave. "This is Gabriel," she said to me. Then she said, "Gabriel, Rose, Rose, Gabriel," and bounced her head back and forth between us.

"Pleased to meet you," Gabriel said. It seemed like we should shake hands at that point, but we already had. The air conditioning in the store was powerful, and I felt goosebumps spreading across my shoulders. "I hear you're training pretty hard," he said. Then he shuffled a little and cleared his throat. "Alexis and I met your timekeeper here on one of our walks. Lexi likes to keep moving too."

I nodded, and Ruby squatted in front of the carriage. She put her fingers on the baby's bare toes. "Hello, little Lexi," she said, using a baby voice I'd never heard her use before. The straps of her bikini were twisted where they wrapped around her back.

"She's so cute," I said. Then I realized all I could see from where I was standing was the top of the carriage and the baby's feet. I tried to remind myself that I was a new person, defined by my competence and strength. I stood there clenching every muscle I could. "We should go," I said to Ruby.

During our walk home, Ruby talked about babies and how she wished we had a baby of our own. "Isn't Lexi the cutest?" she asked me.

A few minutes later she pointed down a side street and said, "That's where Gabriel lives." As we crossed his street, she linked her arm with mine.

☙

Over the next few days, my parents reported significant progress on the house, and I shaved at least five seconds from my mile every time I ran it.

After each run, I'd strip off my clothes and add them to my salty heap in the corner of the bathroom. I'd sweat and sweat until an item was soaked, then toss it on top of the rest. When I had nothing left to wear, I'd wash my heap and start over, like I was building a tower of sweat and rebuilding it again and again.

Every night, I stood in front of the mirror and took stock of myself. My muscles were tightening, pushing to the surface to showcase their strength. All I had to do was admire a particular curve or angle of my body and it became more pronounced, more impressive.

To be capable, all I had to do was feel capable—drop five seconds and five more—whatever I told myself to do.

CR

By the day of the women's gymnastics final, I was consistently running a mile in less than six and a half minutes. I finished my training early that day so that Ruby and I could dedicate the night to the first American gymnasts who had even a chance at beating the Romanians.

All summer we made sandwiches with Philadelphia soft pretzels sawed in two lengthwise. That night we ate them with American cheese, apple slices, and spicy pepperoni. Our choice of ingredients was limited by what was in stock at Wawa, but this restriction only enhanced our culinary imagination.

We had our food ready on our trays for the rebroadcast of an interview with Mary Lou Retton that aired just before the event. We'd seen it twice already, but they'd promised extra footage of her first workout after the knee surgery she had just weeks before. The fact that she'd be competing on a damaged knee sent a spiraling thrill down my spine.

We liked Mary Lou because she was ugly, damaged, and strong. She was America's squat, boy-haired warrior, prepared to launch our country into the gymnastics spotlight. I didn't like her perkiness, but I admired the iron-like force palpable in the thud of her landings. Her love for the games wasn't actually girly at all but domineering and even violent. We had the same fire inside of us, Mary Lou and me. We were graceless and eager to suffer, pounders of the earth, not tiptoers.

I was determined to be a kind of savior once we got to Vermont. I pictured the Russians attacking our new school, all the young Vermontians dressed in brightly colored patchwork, smelling like patchouli, scrambling to me to be saved because I was faster on my feet than anyone for miles around.

They'd strap on roller skates, and I'd be their leader, up front with no skates at all, just my old sneakers and a long rope attached at one end to my waist. I wouldn't have to say a word; they'd grab that rope and I'd pull them to safety—over hills, through rivers and bouncing over rocky creeks, weaving snow-covered pine trees. I'd liberate the rural lot of us, not just from the Russians, but from everything holding us back. I'd lead my people with the sheer strength of my stride.

By the time Mary Lou flipped her second perfect ten on the vault and jumped into the arms of her coach, fists lifted in victory, Ruby and I were practically in tears we were so proud. It was our perfect ten too. It was America's perfect ten. And when we got to Vermont, we'd make our lives a perfect ten.

In that moment, I really believed that both of us thought it was possible.

○য়

The next day Ruby wanted to take a different route home from Wawa. She said she was bored with our usual way of going and convinced me that her alternate route had more hills to challenge my muscles.

I had forgotten about Gabriel until we bumped into him that night. This time he was bare-chested, pacing the sidewalk with Alexis over his shoulder.

He stopped pacing when he saw us. "Good evening, ladies," he said.

Ruby tried to get a look at Lexi, who was hiding her face in Gabriel's shoulder. "Hi, little one," she said, and Gabriel dipped the baby in his arms so we could see her face. She had chubby baby-cheeks that dimpled when she smiled. She didn't seem particularly special.

"My daughter seems to love your sister," Gabriel said to me.

"That's good," I said back. Gabriel had big teeth and an ingratiating smile. There was a thin strip of dark hair on his chest, down the center, and little circles of it surrounding his nipples, which somehow looked more like a woman's than a man's. I felt my pulse speeding up as I noticed these things about him.

"So, what's up with you two tonight?" he asked.

"Nothing at all," Ruby said. She had one foot turned out, that leg and hip pushed forward. It wasn't the way she normally held herself.

"It's a good night for nothing at all," Gabriel said. He smiled, and then he looked confused. "Wait," he said, "which one of you is older?" He was looking back and forth between us, squinting. "You're not twins, are you? I'm kind of obsessed with twins."

I was a couple inches taller than Ruby at the time, but she was more developed; I didn't have much in the way of breasts, and she was already a B-cup. Everyone until Gabriel judged our ages by our heights.

"I'm older," I said, and he made a face like that surprised him.

We had ice cream in our bags and I wanted to keep walking. For all I knew, Gabriel was friends with Mr. Federman. Even in a neighborhood like ours, it was important to be leery of others. It's what my mother had taught us. It's why she trusted us to live alone that summer.

"We've got to get home," I said to Ruby. She had one hand on the baby's leg; she held her other arm out from her body and moved it in tiny circles so that the plastic handles of her bag swung around her wrist. I worried that she might hit the baby with the bag, but I didn't say anything.

"We have ice cream melting," I explained to Gabriel.

"I'm trying to convince Ruby to babysit," Gabriel said to me. Then he repositioned Alexis so her back was pressed to his chest and his chin was resting on her head. "Please," he said to Ruby, like the baby was begging too.

I just stood there and said nothing.

CR

"When did he ask you to babysit?" I asked once we'd turned off Gabriel's street.

"I don't know," Ruby said. "He asked a bunch of times." She was walking with her shoulders back and her chin up. She had a smug expression on her face that made me angry every time I looked at her.

"Why would you want to babysit if you don't have to?" I asked.

She stopped walking and looked at me. "Why are you upset about this?"

"I'm not upset," I told her.

"This isn't a big deal," she said. "Let's just enjoy our night." When she walked off, her ponytail swung back and forth the way ponytails swing on haughty cheerleaders on TV.

"I'm not being uptight," I said to her. "Anyone would worry about you working for that guy." I didn't mean to kick the rock at my feet so hard that it flew up into the air. "I don't think you should babysit for him," I said to her.

"I wouldn't be babysitting for him," she said. "I'd be babysitting for Lexi."

I kicked another rock. I was behind her, but I did it loud enough so she could hear. "You've never taken care of a baby," I reminded her.

"I've babysat with Mom before," she said. "Plus, Lexi loves me."

I tried to calm down. Feeling like the only uptight one in my family only made me feel more uptight. "We're leaving for Vermont in less than a month," I said. "It's not exactly a good time to get attached to some baby."

She stopped walking and turned to face me. "I want this job," she said. Then she walked ahead again, her red flip flops slapping her heels.

"We have to start packing soon," I said. "I need your help at home."

"I think Lexi needs my help a little more than you do," she said. Then she told me that Lexi's mom was dead. She glared at me like it was my fault. Later I learned it wasn't even true—Gabriel just planned to tell Alexis that her mother had died so she wouldn't know she'd been abandoned. I'm pretty sure Ruby knew the truth even then.

"Do you know what most teenagers would be doing if they had the summer to themselves?" she asked. We'd had this conversation many times, but this time felt different, like she'd lost interest in me and didn't want to say it.

"We just have to finish out the summer," I said. "It'll be better in Vermont."

Ruby stood in front of me the way she stood in front of Gabriel, one hip pushed forward and her foot turned out. This time she put her hand on her waist. She was wearing cutoffs with fringe that clung to her thighs. I wanted to tell her go home and put on decent clothing, but I stopped myself. "Our ice cream is melting," I said instead.

For the first time that summer, Wawa was selling Super Fudge Chunk. We'd used the last of our coupons to buy all five pints they had in stock. Who knew what my mother had to do to keep a steady stream of them headed our way.

When we got home, Ruby didn't want to watch TV and eat ice cream like we'd planned. She went into our room and closed the door.

I wanted to go for a run, but my chest felt too tight. I ate two pints of Super Fudge Chunk instead and watched Carl Lewis take the gold in the 100 meters.

After that I gathered all of the photos of the house my mother had sent and spread them on the floor. I tried to arrange them to get a sense of the whole place, but they were too disjointed.

When I called my mother to tell her what I was doing, she acted disappointed in herself for not thinking of it first. *That would have been so much fun for you girls!* she said. Then she complimented me on being so creative and thoughtful to come up with an idea like that. What she didn't tell me was that some of the photos weren't pictures of the house itself, but items she hoped to buy or finishes she'd come across elsewhere and planned to recreate. I was thoughtful enough to figure that out too.

My mother always said that our way of living was the opposite of the religious way: we made our own rules; we weren't suckers waiting for an afterlife to enjoy ourselves. We could choose to enjoy every moment rather than worry about the past or the future. In theory I think it's a great way to live, but I found it hard not to worry that we should be worried.

Ruby spent most of the next six days at Gabriel's. She'd come home in time to have dinner with me and watch an event or two, but it wasn't the same.

She still helped me with my training in the mornings, timing me once or twice, and I'd think of it as my job to improve my speed while she was gone, so I'd have something to show her the next morning. I'd have dinner ready by the time she got home.

Then, on the third day, she came home late for the first time. She came home over an hour late, and she was wearing a dress that belonged to Lexi's mom, an almost see-through dress with strings for straps and just two loose triangles of fabric covering her breasts. She said Gabriel let her wear it because Lexi spit up on her T-shirt and Gabriel was going to wash it for her, but the next day she came home wearing a different dress. According to Ruby, Gabriel's ex left that stuff behind, and he figured someone might as well make use of it.

What made everything weirder is that Gabriel never went anywhere when Ruby was babysitting. Apparently, he wanted company more than a babysitter, which is what I said to Ruby, and she said Gabriel was stuck with the baby—he never wanted a kid and now he was a single father and worked from home and didn't have any co-workers, so Ruby was his co-worker now, and finally Gabriel had someone to complain to. I wanted to ask her what about friends, didn't Gabriel have any friends he could talk to, but I realized it was hypocritical of me to even think that.

"Gabriel likes my company," she said. "Is that so hard to believe?" I pictured her modeling those outfits for Gabriel, stripping and dressing in front of him, though Ruby denied this and rolled her eyes when I mentioned it. All I knew was that she bought new underwear with the money he gave her, and the first time she went out shopping for them was the first time he gave her one of those slinky dresses.

I was also more and more convinced that Gabriel was in touch with Mr. Federman, who, one way or another, was beginning to realize that my parents weren't around. The last time he called and asked for my mother his tone was sarcastic, like he knew there was no point in asking.

Meanwhile, my mother thought it was great that Ruby had gotten a job. When I told her about the dresses, she laughed and said that Ruby was a gorgeous girl and she'd have to learn how to deal with attention from men. She seemed proud more than anything.

To me she said, "Don't worry. Your time will come." Then she told me what she always did, that my beauty was less traditional than Ruby's, and it would take more time for people to recognize and appreciate it.

"Can't we just come to Vermont now?" I asked her.

"Oh, sweetie," she said to me. "I wish you could come this minute so I could give you a big hug." But the house just wasn't ready. She'd been doing little jobs at the motel where they were staying to get their room for almost nothing, but she didn't think they could get a second room right away.

I let her go on and on about the house after that. I didn't tell her that Gabriel had once paid Ruby an extra five dollars to rub a kink out of his neck, and I didn't tell her that Mr. Federman was onto us. I didn't want to hear the optimistic crap she'd say in response.

I loved my mother, so it felt terrible to hate her too.

ʘ

When we hung up, I went outside to sit with Harmony, our neighbors' cat, who was perched on one of our lawn chairs. Harmony wasn't friendly, but I liked talking to her. Sometimes she'd rub against my leg if I held still, but there was an understanding between us that she'd bolt if I ever tried to touch her.

"I'm not beautiful," I said to her as I sat down. She looked at me and then repositioned herself on the chair. "You know what?" I said.

"You're ugly too, and it's not what's important." She jumped from her chair and rubbed her head against my ankle.

It occurred to me that we were both free to roam at will; either of us could take off right then and no one would notice. "Could I ever get you to follow me?" I said down to her.

She purred, like she actually wanted me to pet her, and something about that made me very mad. "Please just let me pet you!" I said. All I did was lower my hand, and she leapt back, hissed, and ran.

I pictured Ruby on the chair next to me or sitting on the kitchen counter as I made dinner. I got a lot of talking done that way, but it wasn't satisfying. I knew Ruby better than anyone in the world, and all I could imagine her saying back to me were slogans or song lyrics.

ೞ

The following Sunday was the first ever women's Olympic marathon. Ruby promised she'd be home in time to see the event from its start, but she wasn't.

That's when I took to the streets. The marathon was my race, a test of conviction and fortitude rather than grace and skill. I kept the TV running and stopped by after each mile to check on American Joan Benoit, who continued to increase her lead. I planned to keep going until I came home to find Ruby there waiting for me.

Then, five rounds in, I bumped into Lauren Goldstein. I was used to running as if no one could see me, so I ran right toward Lauren without realizing it.

She wasn't the worst person I could have seen. We had once been real friends, and though we weren't anymore, she'd recently gained weight, and that seemed to make her nicer and more sensitive. She had her curly hair blown out straight and pulled into a tight ponytail, but there were little curlicues all around her hairline.

"Rose! It's wonderful to see you," she said. She sounded very mature and exactly like her mother. She told me that she and her brother were home from camp because her grandmother was dying, but her tone implied I must have heard this already.

I didn't know what to say, so I smiled and tried to look sad at the same time. I was still out of breath. I could feel sweat pouring out of me everywhere.

The look on Lauren's face was hard to interpret. It was almost loving. "Oh my god, Rosie," she said. "You look so great."

I thought maybe she was joking. I think I apologized. Then I said, "Running makes me really sweaty."

Lauren turned her head and gave me a sideways glance. I wondered if this was the way she looked at boys—it was a little bit scary, but also attractive. Lauren had a reputation for giving handjobs to any boy who wanted one.

"Ethan saw you at Wawa yesterday," she told me. Ethan was Lauren's older brother. Even when Lauren and I were friends, he never said a word to me. Lauren took a step back and looked me up and down. Her smile couldn't have been nicer. "He said you looked hot," she said, but I figured she meant overheated, sweaty.

"I've been running a lot," I told her. I could feel sweat rolling down my neck. The front of my shirt was wet and clinging to me.

"So I see," Lauren said. She said all of this like she was announcing the results of prize she was shocked but pleased to realize I'd won. "Well, honestly, Rose, you look really great."

I didn't know what to say. I didn't like the fact that I had no real friends, but more than that, I didn't like being noticed.

I started to run in place out of nervousness. "I'm actually training right now," I said. Then I said I had to go.

As I ran off, I could feel her behind me, and something about that felt sad. I didn't want to end up like Harmony, too shy and weird to let anyone love me.

I ran as hard as I could. I pictured Ethan and Lauren chasing me; I felt Ethan's eyes on my body, his arms reaching for me. Then I pictured Lauren giving her own brother a handjob.

"I can do whatever I want!" I called out to no one.

I ran faster and faster. In my mind I was stomping over Ethan and Mr. Federman, Jane Fonda, and my own sweaty ineptitude. But I could only go so fast. I was beginning to realize that I wasn't very free or capable at all. I could never be powerful like Carl Lewis or even Ethan Goldstein because I'd always be a girl.

Mary Lou was perky and Jane Fonda wore those pink leotards for the same reason Lauren gave so many handjobs: it was the only option we had.

Another fact: I should have been thrilled that someone like Ethan Goldstein said something nice about me, but I wished he hadn't. I wasn't running to attract that kind of attention, and I hated that Lauren assumed I was.

In my mind I was explaining all of this to Ruby as I ran, but even in my own head I couldn't get her to understand what I was trying to say.

ରଙ

When I got back to the garage, Mr. Federman was there waiting for me.

As soon as I stopped running I could hear my heart beating in my ears. It was hard to hear anything else. "You know your TV is on," is I think what he said to me. He pointed through the window. I had sweat in my eyes. He looked like he was swaying in front of me.

"Sorry," I said.

Mr. Federman was wearing a gray suit and shiny black shoes. He shook his head, but then he looked at me and smiled. "Good run?" he asked.

I couldn't say anything because I was trying to catch my breath. I could feel my fingertips tingling.

He looked through the window again and then back at me. "Where's your mother?" he asked.

I wanted to think of an answer that would save us. This was my moment to do it, but I was exhausted and it felt impossible. "Gone," I told him.

Mr. Federman rubbed his palms together, like he was brushing off crumbs. He was either angry or he pitied me, and I couldn't decide which would be worse.

"She's coming home soon," I said. I wanted it to be true. I wanted my mother to run up to us right then and tell him we didn't need his pity or his stupid garage because she'd built us a beautiful home in Vermont. I wanted him to see how impressive she was.

"When exactly is she coming home?" he asked. Drops of sweat were falling from my face. "Are you okay?" he asked me.

For a second I felt like a small child, like it wasn't sweat on my face but tears that I couldn't hold in any longer. I felt like I was lost and he'd found me. Then everything felt very quiet and still. "I'll have her call you tonight," I said to him.

Mr. Federman smiled and put out his hand, but I wouldn't take it. "I'm too sweaty," I told him.

"Okay," he said. He put his hand on my shoulder quickly, and then pulled back. "I'm sorry to have stopped by unannounced," he said.

"It's okay," I managed to say. "I understand."

He stood with his hands in his pockets, blocking my way to the door. "Are you sure you're okay?" he asked me. "Ruby?" he said, thinking that was my name.

I didn't know how to answer him, so I didn't say anything. I clenched my teeth to keep myself from crying.

"I do need to hear from your mother tonight," he said. He bent his knees a little, so he was closer to my height. He raised his eyebrows. "Tonight," he said again. Then he said, "Goodbye, Ruby. Please take care of yourself."

I watched him walk to his car and pictured Greg Lougainis on the high dive, standing in silence, his arms outstretched, all of his strength and hard work on display for the world. It's what I thought I wanted—to stand valiant and victorious over everyone else. But there was something terrible about him standing up there like that, all alone.

"Wait!" I called out to Mr. Federman, but the wind was blowing and there was a truck passing on the street and he couldn't hear me. "Wait," I said again. I thought about running after him, wrapping my arms around him from behind and resting my hot face on his clean suit, letting my sweat soak into the fabric. I just wanted to hug him for a second, even though I hated him.

"Wait," I said one more time, but by that point, he was already driving away.

My Husband Story

In their bedroom, on the second floor of their two-bedroom house in the suburbs, the woman kneeled over her husband, who was lying on his back in their bed.

She put his left toe to sleep first, the most-left of his left toes. Then she moved onto the others: "Bigger, bigger, bigger, biggest," she said. "You have to give yourself permission to turn off each part, like we're freeing your body from its usual responsibilities."

Their ten-day beach vacation was scheduled to begin that night. "You need a nap before we leave," she had told her husband.

"Now turn off your ankles," she said, and he did.

"I really can't feel them," he said. "It's like they're made of wet clay." He smiled, like he was only kidding. "I'm ready for my calves," her husband said—that's how willing he was.

He lay in his usual sleeping spot, holding still for her. "This is amazing," he said, gazing up at the woman. "Seriously. You're amazing." This he said like he wasn't kidding.

She moved slowly up his legs, onto his hips and torso. "You don't even need these," the woman said as she put his little nipples to sleep. He didn't like to have his nipples touched. It did nothing for him.

She saved his head and private parts for last. He did everything she told him to do. He liked to be dominated by her. He'd made this clear. Even when they reached his chin he had a smile on his face.

She gave him a kiss on his lips before putting his mouth to sleep. "Next your tongue," she said. "Any last words?" He nodded sleepily and smiled. She thought about the sand at the beach where they'd rented a small, two-person cabin. Inside, from the pictures at least, it looked like a cabin you'd find in the forest, with dark wood furniture and thick burgundy drapes. It was going to be their first vacation together. She imagined putting her husband to sleep outside in the sand, slipping his body down into it, covering him. He could enjoy the sun and sand and she could have time alone in the cool dark cabin.

She caressed his cheek, then put it to sleep too. "Off?" she said, and he blinked yes, then closed his eyes.

Every part of him was asleep, except for his cock, which had become swollen and hard, calling her attention to it. *Don't forget me!* it seemed to be saying.

She reached her hand into his pants and held him in her fist, rubbing him the way he liked to be rubbed, the way the line of ex-girlfriends behind her had touched him, probably. But no other part of his body responded. She unzipped his pants and pulled it out. She lowered her lips to the tip of it. "Okay, this too," she said, and she felt it slowly falling limp into sleep.

A breeze came like a wave through their bedroom window, cooling and comforting their skin. She leaned closer to her husband. "I love you," she said, and then laid down next to him. He was asleep the first time she admitted she was in love with him. She whispered *I love you* into his sleeping back for months before actually telling him to his face.

"You're my husband," she said now. "We're in bed together. This is our bed, and I love you." She gave him a kiss on the forehead and it didn't wake him.

"I'm not really powerful," she said to their bedroom ceiling. "I'm actually very scared." She turned toward him and buried her face in his neck. She draped her body over his. "I'm not brave," she said, "And I'm not ready."

A week before this, the woman's husband had said to her: *I care about you more than anything, do you know that?*

"Now I'll try to put myself to sleep," she said. "I think I can do it if you promise you'll stay asleep. I want to do synchronized sleeping with you. Just for a while. Just until I'm ready."

She lay on her side, facing him. She draped her arm over him and pressed her chest into his shoulder. She tried to turn off her smallest left toe, to let it off the hook. She turned away from him. She took a deep breath. Her online meditation teacher had a soft, British voice, and she could hear it instructing her the way she'd instructed her husband. She pictured her body and her husband's body, sleeping and then waking in unison, flying side-by-side to their two-person cabin on the coast.

But she couldn't sleep.

ଔ

The woman scoured their kitchen and scrubbed their floors. It would be nice to come home to a clean house. She put their suitcases by the door. When she went back to the bedroom, her husband was still sleeping. She tapped him on the shoulder and then shook him, but he didn't wake up.

"I wanted you asleep and now you are," she said. She felt like a child discovering she had a secret, magic power. "You're here and not here," she said.

She climbed onto the bed and stood over him. It was better than watching him from afar, that feeling she got when she watched through the window as he walked off to work or got a glimpse of him farther out in the world, one person among other people, and she'd look at him and think: *That's my husband. That's MY husband.*

"What should we do?" she asked him, bouncing on the bed. "We can do anything!"

She leapt to the floor and landed in a knees-bent, arms-out

surfer pose. She was facing her closet. "Actually, I should get organized first," she said. "Let's go," she said. "Let's do this."

When she told her mother that she planned to get married, her mother said, *You'll be fine. Just treat him like you used to treat your stuffed animals.*

"What's in my closet?" the woman asked aloud and rhetorically. "Well, that's what we're about to find out!"

Her husband had a slight smile on his face. "I am a magician and you are my audience," she said to him. She still wasn't convinced he was really asleep.

"Restart," she said. "Take two." She moved closer to the bed and leaned down over him. "Hello, and welcome to my channel!" she said at full volume. Then she stood upright and addressed a more general, nonexistent audience. "I know, I know. I'm not the type to have a channel, but this is my channel. Today we are going to clean out my closet. I'd like to get rid of anything ugly. What makes something ugly? I have no idea, but I want to find out. Just a minute," she said.

She closed the door to the bedroom behind her and the door to the bathroom once she was in there. She pictured a camera continuing to film the empty space in front of her closet. The camera would pick up the sound of her husband breathing in bed, but nothing else.

You're alone, she whispered to herself, but she locked the bathroom door and let the water run. *Are any of you cancer cells?* she said quietly to the bloody toilet paper. *Now's a good time to announce yourself.*

ରୟ

"Step one," she said, back on her mark, and pulled everything out of her closet. "You're lucky you get to see this," she said. "Some channels won't show the process. Everyone loves a montage of before and after photos, sure, but how is that helpful? See my husband?

That's my husband, in my bed. He's sleeping. Right, Honey? I never call him Honey—do I, Honey?"

On the top of one pile was the faded Captain America T-shirt her brother had called his lucky T-shirt and wore nonstop, it seemed, during the year he spent dying of cancer. It was there in the pile, like all the other T-shirts.

There were so many items heaped in front of her, like mountains blocking her way to the bed. "This is not a good show. I'm too tired," she said. "Why do you get to sleep?"

She turned her back to the camera that wasn't there, pulled off her sundress and bra and replaced them with a stretched-out tank top and a pair of loose terrycloth shorts. She climbed over the piles and into the bed. "If my life partner were still a cat," she said, "I could wear this outfit all the time. You know what I'm really in the mood to do? Watch Animal Planet."

She propped her husband into a seated position. "I'm looking for the otter episode of *That's My Baby!*, if you must know." Her husband's head had lolled slightly to the left. "Hello?" she said. "Did you hear that? We're going to watch Animal Planet all day." It was quiet in the room. Outside, the occasional bird chirped. She heard the rumbling whoosh of a car passing by. "The otter is by far the saddest episode of *That's My Baby!* It's not as stupid as you're assuming," she told her husband.

Another car rolled past, driven by someone she didn't know, someone who probably hadn't even glanced at their house. "It's a stillbirth," she said. "I'm not spoiling anything because you're sleeping and you can't hear me. Right?"

The woman put her hand on her husband's back and pushed his torso forward until she could no longer see his face. His hair was very short in the back. "They don't know how to deal with the mother," the woman said, "because she won't let go of the baby. They have to decide how long to wait before pulling it away from her. They try to distract her with food, to get her to drop it, but that doesn't work. She just swims and swims in circles around the birthing pool, clutching her dead baby. The handlers say that she knows it's dead, but you'll have to judge for yourself. Okay?"

The woman searched and searched, but she couldn't find the otter episode. "They have every puppy episode, the wobbly newborn giraffe with its delightfully weak legs, countless cutesy kittens, but no otter." The woman wedged her body behind her husband's, her legs straddling his hips. She pulled him upright so that her chest pressed into his back. "Otters swim on their backs," she whispered. "It's the only way they can swim. It's a special thing about them. I remember the mother trying to flip over, like she's trying to hide her baby under her, under the water, so they won't take it from her, but she can't control her body—she just spins around onto her back again and again. I don't know which is sadder, if she knows it's dead the whole time, or if it's sadder to watch and wait for her to realize it's dead. It was her first baby, and she's just an otter, so there's really no saying what she understood."

The woman pulled off her husband's T-shirt and kissed his bare skin. "Your shoulder smells good, and I like your freckles," she said. She wasn't very good at compliments. She wanted to get better at it. "I want to go on our vacation," she told her husband.

The room was such a mess. "Fucking wake up," she said. "I need your help." His back rose and fell with his breath, steady and slow, like he hadn't a care in the world.

"Ever worry that you'll never get organized?" she said to the freckles on her husband's back. She pictured disorganized clumps of cancer growing inside of her, pushing at her organs and squeezing between her bones, stretching her skin like boulders.

Nothing ever felt completely good. There was always something in the way.

"Maybe she thought all babies were born still," the woman said. "Maybe she thought she was supposed to swim around that way to get it moving. Maybe she blamed herself and thought she wasn't swimming fast enough. I don't remember how it ends," the woman said. "I wish I could remember."

Eventually, the otter's dead baby would start to smell. It wasn't something they mentioned. Would the mother let go at that point? "I do feel lonely," the woman said to her husband, "but I feel like

I need to be alone to get the feeling to pass. Have you ever felt that way?"

⚮

When it was time for them to leave for the airport, the woman said to her husband, "If you don't wake up this minute, we're not going. Open your eyes," she said. "I mean it."

The woman's husband shifted slightly in the bed, but he did not take the dare. He looked happy to be sleeping. "Who are you?" she asked him. "Do you ever feel like you're only ever talking to yourself?"

She put her hand on his shoulder. It was a relief to realize she couldn't accidentally wake him. She rubbed his soft, blondish-red hair. "I made us miss our vacation," she said. "Are you angry? Why do you never get angry? What could I do to make you so mad you'd hit me? There must be something." He had two small freckles on his earlobe that she had never noticed before. "You could be anyone," she said, "but you're my husband. You're my family. This is what people do. They get married and make families." She touched his stubbly cheek. "Where are you?" she asked. "Are you still in there? Are you mad? Do you think you'll ever want to wake up?" She pulled up his shirt and looked at his chest. "Hello?" she said to its flatness. "I have no idea who you are. It's time to open your eyes." But he wouldn't or couldn't.

⚮

So the woman went back to cleaning. She made a show of dusting and scrubbing and taking care of their things.

She put on her bathing suit and an apron and did a cooking

show for him. She brought all the ingredients into the bedroom. She propped him up and put a tray on his lap.

She pretended she was on the Food Network, a woman cooking for her husband who wouldn't wake up. *Will this recipe convince him to wake up? Was she even trying?*

Then it wasn't the food network but her own network. She designed the sets and created every single show. *Today she's going to wax his chest hair! Will he wake up to stop her? She's shaving her own head! She's wearing a leotard and legwarmers and simultaneously choreographing and performing her own aerobics routine!* Instead of commercials, she took before and after shots of her and her husband. *Here's my stomach before I ate all the cookies in the house, and here it is now! Presto change-o!*

છ

"Let's let some sunshine in," she said to her husband once it was morning. The leaves on the tree outside their bedroom window were just beginning to turn yellow. Soon they'd have to rake. Then shovel. Then cut the grass and water the lawn and then rake again, and then shovel. There was so much to do, but there was the sun, just shining away.

The sun sets, another day is gone. The sun rises, another day begins. *You can't have more time*, it seemed to be saying. *I cause cancer and make plants grow.* The woman looked over at her husband. *Ready or not*, the sun was saying.

The woman closed the curtain and climbed into the bed. She felt very tired. "I want to protect you," she said to her husband. "Whatever I've done to you, I'm going to fix it." She got on top of him and hugged him with her arms and legs and tucked her head in the crook of his neck.

That's when she noticed he was smaller.

With her head on his collar bone, she could almost touch his ankles with her toes. She felt fear gush through her body like hotter, faster-moving blood. She held him tighter. She could hold more of him than she ever could. "I want to hold all of you," she whispered into his ear. She squeezed him tighter, slipped her hands through the armholes in his T-shirt. That's when she discovered the tiny patch of fur between his shoulder blades. She felt her love for him flash like something electric inside of her.

❧

The next morning she woke to find that her husband had light orange fur on his arms and legs instead of hair. His finger and toe-nails were curled and pointed. She found tiny triangular ears on either side of his head.

He was small enough that she was able to move him into the room they used for storage, behind stacks of boxes and racks of clothing. She covered his body with a blanket.

"Sometimes," she said, "it's best to start by proving to yourself that you're strong and capable, even if you're pretty sure you're not." She pulled on her heaviest winter boots and her winter coat and snow pants and ran up and down their steps until she was dripping sweat, then she ran faster. "Nobody look," she said. "This is training for the show, not part of it." She'd read an article about muscle burn that said it's only a warning. Even when you feel like you can't possibly push yourself any harder, you're nowhere near muscle failure. "I'm fine," she said to herself. "I'm capable."

When she returned to the storage room, her husband was still asleep. His spine seemed to have curved, and the shape of his face had triangulated.

In the corner of the storage room was a multilevel cat tower, still covered in fur, pinned with almost invisible shards of cat claw. She gave up her cat when her husband moved in because he was allergic to cats. Her mother said it was the right thing to do. The cat spent most of his kittenhood hiding in the dark, enclosed compartment at the base of that tower. But the woman had turned him into a lap cat. She convinced him that was a better way to be. Then she was annoyed by how often he wanted to sit in her lap. Then she gave him away.

The woman stood over her husband, watching the rise and fall of his breath. When she kneeled at his side, he started to purr. She wanted to pet his head, but it seemed wrong. She couldn't just love him when she felt like it and then change her mind.

A tree branch, pushed by the wind, scraped the storage room window. If her husband were awake, he would have insisted on trimming the branch to protect their house. He'd lean his long body out their window and trim the tree to protect them. She looked at the branch, at the big world outside their house. The wind was whipping and whistling, and her husband was sleeping and purring on the floor.

೧

Four days later, the woman's husband was small enough to hold like a child over her shoulder. "You were so big," she said to him. "I liked that about you. I miss the length and weight of you. But this is nice too." She bounced him gently in her arms and rubbed the soft fur on his back.

There was a part of her that wanted her husband to stay exactly like this: half-man, half-cat. It felt safe and manageable.

"Just kidding," she said into her husband's little cat ear. "I know you can't hear my thoughts, but just in case you can, don't worry. I'll get things back to the way they were. And remember, I'm a woman. What I want is mostly irrelevant. My thoughts and behavior are barely connected."

The woman had not showered in four days. She lifted her arm and positioned her husband so that her armpit was pressed to his dry little cat nose. Was his sense of smell heightened in his current state? She reminded herself that smells aren't good or bad to cats. She'd read that. Cats don't moralize scents the way humans do.

When the phone rang, it startled her, and she dropped him. He dug his claws into her skin but couldn't hold on. The phone only rang once, but the feeling of panic lingered. She watched her husband curl himself into a ball on the floor. The parts of him that were still human looked grotesque, over-sized and hairless, like tumors.

The woman gazed outside. Someone would have to walk right up to their window and peer down to see her husband where he was on the floor. The scratches on her shoulder and arm burned and bled. "Sometimes I feel like I hate you," she said to her husband. "Sometimes I think I wouldn't care if you died." She crouched down to get a better look at him. She had always admired the look of orange cats, but they seemed like the kind of cat other people would have. "You still feel like a stranger," she told him. "I mean, even before this." He rolled over and tucked his head under his arm, but it didn't seem to be a reaction to what she was saying. "Our brains are out of our control," she said. "I can't help it if I hate you sometimes, and I can't control whether or not you absorb what I'm saying. I wish I could, but I just can't." Her husband started to purr. "I don't want you in my house," she said. Then she clarified, "I'm only kidding," just in case he could understand her.

◌

Three times a day, she opened her husband's mouth and put a wintergreen mint on his tongue. She held her breath when she did this, not because his breath smelled bad but because she worried it might.

She kept him in the bed for most of the day, letting him rest. She brushed his fur and wiped guck from his eyes. "Please know that I don't ever want to be put in hospice," she told him. "But I don't want you dealing with me yourself. Do you understand?" Her husband scratched behind his ear but continued sleeping. "If your bodily functions are out of your control, that should be your own problem. I'm not talking about you. I really do enjoy taking care of you like this," she said and pressed her head to his.

At thirty-four years old, the woman's body was changing in ways she couldn't reliably track. The more she brushed her teeth to keep them from offending anyone, the more brittle they would become, the more likely to decay.

Her husband's body had become more flexible. It bent the way a cat's body bends. She picked him up and took him outside, into their backyard. It was dark and surrounded by trees. "Do you really feel for me what men feel for their wives?" she asked her husband.

She imagined her body dying in hospice, propped up on pretty pillows, floral blankets hiding her gray skin, the mucus and decay inside of her. She'd rather bury herself alive than allow that to happen. But then what? She'd be buried and her husband wouldn't be able to find her. He'd be sad because he couldn't say goodbye.

She didn't find out that her cat had died until a month after it happened. No one thought to tell her. He was taken to the vet and put down before he had the chance to crawl away and hide himself. It was her fault. She gave him to a man who lived in a high-rise apartment in the city. The cat had nowhere to hide.

"I shouldn't have married you," she said to her husband. "I'm sorry." Their backyard was too small for her to dig a hole for herself without him noticing. She had no place to hide herself either.

ѯ

The next afternoon, the woman put her husband into the backpack they'd planned to bring to the beach. It was just big enough to fit her husband's little body as long as she put his still-human parts in first, his big feet and hands, bending his smaller but human-shaped legs and tucking his furry head between them. She left the zipper open enough to slip her hand inside. She kissed her fingers and pressed them into the leopard spotted fur that lined his spine. "I'm going to take you for a walk, my little Honey," she said.

Sometimes she felt like the two of them were starring in a horror movie. The woman was the psychopath in a trench coat with knives strapped to her body, and her husband was the skinny blonde girl, braless in a perfect white tank top.

Outside, the clouds were pretty white puffs and the sky was sky-blue. The trees were tall and colorful, the air chilly but not cold. The woman could feel the warmth of her husband's body against her back, through the canvas of the bag and the cotton of her clothes. At the end of their street was an unpaved road that led to a park with a pond.

Her husband's body jostled against her back as she walked. It felt like he was reaching out to her, or wanting to, like the spark of desire in a paraplegic—strong, but invisible. She wanted to walk with the backpack against her chest, but there was something liberating about leaving it where it was, something exciting about resisting the urge, just letting him bounce behind her.

When she got to the park, she sat on a bench by the pond and held her husband in the bag on her lap. She watched ducks pit-pat in pairs on the pond.

The sun was out again. Children played on the jungle gym at the side of the park. Their caretakers stood around the perimeter of the playground with strollers and smartphones. When the kids called *Look!*, they looked. The woman stared straight at the pond, but she could see the children's brightly-colored clothing like psychedelic swirls out of the corner of her eye.

Humans and apes were the only animals who liked to be looked at. She'd read that. She reached her hand into her backpack and rubbed her husband's head. She could feel the vibrating purr of his body in the bag. "Look at me," she whispered, but it made her nervous to say it. Was she ever like those kids? Was she ever a normal human? She couldn't remember. "Let's just relax," she said to her husband. She felt a bit calmer out in the world, like whatever they were doing didn't matter very much.

It was the woman's idea to go to the beach for vacation. She had looked forward to the water. She'd thought a lot about the feeling of the water and waves on her skin. She had a brand new bathing suit packed in the very backpack that now held her husband. They were going to go into the water together.

ᆼ

On her way home from the park, the woman called her sister.

"Are you at the beach?" her sister asked.

The woman stopped walking. She imagined a gaping hole in the ground in front of her, and in that hole was the beach vacation. "We didn't go," she told her sister. There was warmth and brightness at the bottom of that hole, but all the woman could feel was the empty darkness she'd have to fall through to get there.

"Are you in the car?" she asked. Her sister often called as she drove from the school where she taught to the school her children attended. It was just a fifteen-minute drive, but it was the only time she had privacy. There was one spot, about ten minutes into the ride, where she almost always lost reception and had to call back.

"I'm in the car, but there's traffic," her sister said. "Tell me what happened. I have time."

"Work emergency," the woman said about her husband. "He figured it'd be less stressful for both of us if he stayed and got his work done."

"Sounds like Mom," her sister said. The woman had forgotten that she'd spent the weeks leading up to their vacation worrying that something would come up at work and he'd cancel. But he hadn't actually canceled on her for work in a long time. His priorities had changed.

"If you could be any animal, which animal would you want to be?" the woman asked her sister. She tightened the straps on her backpack and picked up her pace. It looked like it was going to rain.

"You sound sad," her sister said. "Do you want to hang out tomorrow? I could cut a couple of classes and hang out with you."

The woman felt her husband shift in the bag on her back. *Does love ever feel to you like a gaping hole in your chest?* she wanted to ask her sister.

Instead, she said, "I've been thinking about the fact that animals run away to hide when they're dying. They're animals. Why would they be ashamed?"

Her sister laughed. "That's not why," she said. "You're projecting."

"So why do they hide?" the woman asked. Her sister was a science teacher. She tended to accept that certain things were unknowable. The woman felt something inside her relax. Maybe all of her assumptions were wrong, and it would make sense to just stop thinking.

"Hold on," her sister said. "I have to focus on turning. Okay, sorry," she said. "It's because of predators. They hide because they know they're weak and can't defend themselves."

"Oh," the woman said. "That makes sense."

"So I guess you don't want to get together?" her sister said.

When he was in hospice, their brother used his bedpan with everyone there in his room. After her sister gave birth, their father sent group emails to everyone in the family, detailing the gas her body was producing and passing. Her sister wasn't even cc'd on those emails. Humans were so big, and there was so much guck in them.

∞

The day they were scheduled to return from their vacation, the woman sat by the window in their storage room with her husband in her lap. She pet him in all the places he liked to be pet. Not the places he liked to be touched when he was human, not the places his exes knew about. He was entirely cat now, but still sleeping.

Everything in their house felt quiet and comfortable. There was a slight breeze coming through the window. Her husband was purring in her lap. Their life felt good this way. Manageable.

Then the woman glanced across the street. She looked into the neighbor's yard, and there was her husband, her fully-human husband, raking the neighbor's lawn. He was wearing the blue T-shirt she gave him, the one he always wore when he tended to their yard.

The woman was about to yell out the window, *What are you doing? That's not our lawn!* But then she saw him wave to Maureen, who was inside her house across the street, who was also looking out the window. She saw Maureen wave at her husband and felt the cat stir in her lap. The cat stretched his front legs and kneaded her hip with his claws. Her husband and Maureen had dopey loving smiles on their faces. *I don't have that smile in my repertoire*, the woman thought. She felt the stick of claws in her side and a burning sensation in her stomach.

She pet the cat behind his ears, hoping that would lull him back to sleep, but he shook his head. He jumped from her lap onto the windowsill. He stared like a predator at her husband across the street and hissed. "Stop it!" the woman yelled. "Don't hiss at him. Just stay quiet." But the cat wouldn't stop hissing.

When the woman tried to grab him, the cat slid through her hands and leapt onto the branch outside the window. He scurried down the tree into the leaves that covered her front lawn. She watched her husband, across the street, look over and smile his smile at the woman's cat.

She felt exposed, like the cat was a part of herself that she should never let anyone see.

But she was inside her house. She hid behind the curtain and no one could see her. She peeked through her window and watched the cat run across the street toward her husband.

She felt a great desire for both of them, a kind of deep satisfaction as the cat moved closer and then pressed its nose to her husband's leg. "Wait, don't! He's allergic!" the woman screamed quietly, but apparently, now that her husband was living across the street with Maureen, tending to their lawn, his allergy was gone.

The woman stuck her head halfway out the window. She was about to call for them. *Come home!* she was going to yell, as loud as she could. But just as she was about to open her mouth, it started to rain, pouring down on the whole neighborhood, and she watched her husband kneel and lift the cat in his arms.

Maureen was standing in the doorway across the street, and she yelled to them before the woman had a chance. "Come in!" Maureen yelled, "Come in!" Her voice was kind and welcoming, not overly-angry and nuts. The woman watched her husband run to Maureen with the cat in his arms. She watched Maureen reach out for them. Maureen was laughing and her husband was laughing and even the cat looked like it was laughing. "Come in, come in, come in," Maureen said, and she shut the door behind them.

ℭ℟

That night, the woman dreamt that it was all a dream, that in reality she and her husband and the cat lived together.

"You believed that I was asleep all that time?" her husband says and laughs in the dream. He kisses her neck and hugs her. She is bald, and he kisses her bald head, holds it gently in his big hands like a delicate and beautiful egg. He's still allergic to the cat, but he wants her to be happy so he agrees to keep it.

The woman presses herself against her husband's big, warm body. "I dreamt that you weren't mine anymore," she says. "You lived across the street. You loved Maureen. You smiled at her. It was easy. It was easier than being with me." She's about to ask, *Would you prefer that? Who are you?* but instead, she holds onto him as tightly as she can, so grateful it feels like her body is going to burst apart with the intensity of it, like holding onto her husband is the only way to keep her fragile head from cracking open and making a mess.

They kiss and kiss in their bed.

But then something woke her, another clap of thunder. When she opened her eyes, she was alone in the bed, the only breathing being in the whole house.

ℭ℟

In the middle of that night, the woman walked to her bedroom window and looked outside. In the moonlight, she could see her husband standing in the leaves on her lawn, looking up at her. "Just making sure you're okay. I'll let you be," he said, and he turned his back to the woman and walked across the street.

If I Could Have Anything,
I'd Only Choose This

This is how it works: When I am with Helen, I can have Hopscotch and Butterscotch with me too, but I cannot acknowledge them when Helen is there. Helen is my real sister, and Butterscotch is my alternate sister. Hopscotch is the alternate me.

When I say that I don't acknowledge Hop and Butter, what I mean is that I don't acknowledge them in any way that Helen could notice. For example, if I am sitting on the couch watching TV with Helen, Butter can sit on the floor with her back against my legs, and if I want to talk to Butter, I don't have to actually talk—I just hold my fist to my mouth and that's our microphone and because Butter is my alternate sister, she can hear me. When Butter talks, I put my fist to my ear, but I make it look like I'm just rubbing my face with my fist because it itches or like I'm holding my fist to my face because I'm being thoughtful.

When Butter is down by my feet I don't have to worry about what's going to happen next because Butter wraps her arms around my legs and I hold my fist to my ear and she says, "You're okay—I'm here. You're Hop. You don't have to worry."

When she says that, I turn into Hop. First I feel a bullet racing around my body that is filled with the happy, buzzing feeling of being Hop, and then that feeling spreads everywhere and my feet turn into Hop's cute, pink, little feet and then up through my legs and torso and then my whole body is my alternate, perfect and tiny body of Hop.

When Helen is focused on her TV show, I keep Hop at my side on the couch so I can remind myself that she's there, with her very skinny legs against my actual legs, like I can choose to have her legs instead of my legs whenever I want.

☙

When Hop's body is against my body and Helen is there in the room, the sensation is both magical and real: the best me is attached to the actual me and I am both of us at once.

I should explain that sometimes I am Hopscotch, and sometimes I watch Hopscotch. It took me a while to realize that this was the case. I like it best when I am Hopscotch, but sometimes I have to enjoy her from the outside in order to make it even better once I am inside Hop.

Sometimes the barriers between the two aren't as clear as I'm making them sound. Sometimes I'm inside and outside at the same time.

I never imagine that I am Butterscotch. Sometimes I let myself imagine what it would be like to be Helen, to get to live in her body and to know what her thoughts are like, but I want none of this from Butter. I just want Butter to exist, and I want her right by me, like a human pillow or a blanket that I can hug or curl up under. If I ever imagine that I'm inside Butter, it's more like I'm wrapped up inside her, but I'm still me, or I'm Hop, or both, and then we're protected because Butter blocks us from everything and hides us. I really don't want to know what that's like for Butter. Just the idea of it makes me feel guilty and nervous and ruins the whole point of Butter.

If I do not pass fifth grade, I have to get rid of Hop and Butter entirely. This is my number-one rule right now. I cannot be the oldest and dumbest person in my grade and still have Hop and Butter.

My biggest fear is that my mother is going to have the new baby on exactly the same day that I have to take my end-of-the-year tests at school. Both are supposed to happen in just two weeks, and I'm worried that when I'm taking my tests, my mother will be so focused on the new baby that I'll fail.

What I like to imagine is that it's Hop inside my mother's belly, and when the new baby is born, I will disappear and become Hop entirely, as a new baby, starting over from the beginning. That's really what I want more than anything.

Sometimes Hop and Butter like to sneak into Helen's room when she's sleeping. Helen sleeps in just short shorts and a tank top, so you really see a lot of her, especially if you're patient and wait for her to roll into different positions.

The actual me only goes into Helen's room if she's not home. When she is home, I can only stare at her until I count to three, and only if she's not looking at me. When Helen catches me staring it's worse than not getting to stare at all.

In the special afternoon school that the actual me has to attend every Tuesday and Thursday, we do mindfulness and emotion regulation. The teacher tells us to imagine a place where we feel safe and happy and there's sunlight everywhere. The teacher says, "Imagine that the sunlight is melting away any tension that you feel." I always imagine that the sunlight is melting my actual body and stretching my bones long and lean until I am in Helen's body and in her bed with my own tank top twisted around my torso and my ribs showing the way Helen's ribs show when she twists that way.

But the truth is that every single part of Helen's body looks different from every part of mine. Helen is like a natural blonde, but with her whole body. She has smooth, glowing yellow light inside of her. Everything about her is a tan sun-kissed glow stretched long and lean.

What I'd really like to do is take Helen's body into my own room and lay her on my bed and remove all her clothes so that I can look at every inch of her body and spend as much time as I need comparing every inch of her body to every inch of mine. But even then I wouldn't know everything that I want to know because there are so many interfering factors—for example, our age difference.

I wish I could have a copy of Helen's body at every age she's been, like one of those wooden dolls where you have the little dolls tucked inside the bigger dolls. I wish I could have all the Helens like this, one tucked inside the next inside the next, and I could look at whichever one I wanted whenever I wanted for the rest of my life, except then it wouldn't really be Helen, so it wouldn't be interesting.

It's all much easier if I'm Hop. Hop is even skinnier than Helen, so it makes me less anxious if I can compare myself as Hop to Helen and have Butter there to tell me it's not even good to be as skinny as I am when I'm Hop.

As soon as they enter Helen's room, Hop goes to the farthest corner of the room and hides while Butter gets up into the bed with sleeping Helen. Even when Helen is not in her bed, Helen's bed smells like Helen.

If I get anxious, Butter says, *Remember, you can count*, and then I count my breaths: in is one, out is two, in is three, out is four, until I get to ten—after that Butter is back to strong-Butter in Helen's bed and Hop is safe in the corner because Butter is strong.

Then I connect Butter's eyes to Hop's eyes so that Hop can see what Butter sees up close and Butter can see Hop's body up close. This way Hop can stay in the corner and Butter can still compare Hop's body to Helen's body.

If Hop gets impatient and wants a quicker, more exact comparison than Butter is willing to do, then Hop has to get into the bed too, in the exact same position as Helen, so that Butter can be sure that every part of Hop is skinnier than every part of Helen.

Luckily, Butter can tell when Hop is getting too nervous for her own good, and then she swoops Hop up in her arms as if Hop is as light as a sheet of paper, and she closes Hop's whole body up in her hand until Hop is all warm sensation and isn't thinking anymore. Then Butter brings Hop back to me in my bed and I get to be Hop.

Sometimes it's hard for me to feel like I'm Hop after thinking about Helen, especially if I think about the fact that Helen is in the bedroom right next mine. Then I feel not like Hop at all, and Hop has to run circles around my bed and slap her knuckles against my walls and throw herself on the ground as hard as she can while Butter begs her to please relax and get into the bed so that Butter can comfort us. When Hop is flinging herself against my walls, she is as tiny and girlish as she ever is, and she wears soft pajamas with the thinnest pink stripes, like baby girl pajamas, but they still hang off of her because she's so skinny.

I should admit that the actual me, during this time, is almost always just lying on my back too lazy to run and fling myself the way Hop does. This is why it takes so long to give in and relax, because I'm already relaxing so I don't deserve to relax.

It used to be that as soon as I started crying I'd let Butter comfort me, but now I wait for as long as I can and I have to clench all of my muscles until I get at least one cramp, and it has to be a painful one, and it takes not just crying but getting out of breath from crying. I have to really exhaust myself and only then can I be Hop and curl up on Butter. That's the only way it feels good, like it couldn't have been earned any more than it was.

Then Butter says, "It's okay, you're Hop, you're Hop," and Butter is all around me and my whole body is my tiny girl Hop body and I can breathe without having to count my breaths because Butter says if they need to be counted, she'll count them. "Just sleep," she says. She is everywhere and she whispers words in my ears until I am almost asleep and then she just breathes in my ears and my bedsheets are soft and pink and striped and they are mine.

Right before we fall asleep is the one time Hop and I are completely one.

തദ

When I am at my desk at school, I am not allowed to pretend that I am Hop and I am not allowed to have Butter. If I start to want Hop and Butter, I have to picture them on the top shelf of my cold metal locker, shoved to the back, covered in all of my terrible tests with my terrible grades on them, most of which I have not yet shown to my mother. I make myself picture my exact grade on each and every test, in Ms. Rubin's exact handwriting, next to my stupid name in my stupid handwriting. If I want to think about Hop and Butter I have to think about those tests instead because that's what I should be thinking about.

If I try all the techniques I know and I still can't focus on my work, I am allowed to imagine Butter hugging Hop, but I have to picture Butter's nice soft body pressed really hard into the back metal wall of my locker, so that it hurts Butter to comfort Hop, and I have to imagine that Hop is a boy—as different from the actual me as Hop ever is—with his boney boy knees pulled to his chest and his skinny boy arms covered in goosebumps, and Butter kissing his arms and his knees and then just wrapping herself around him so that her body is the only body touching any part of the cold metal, and it can only be from the outside that I am watching them, through the small slats at the top of my locker, and the only way I can get inside to be Hop is to focus on my work and improve my performance at school and get high grades and replace all of the failing tests with good tests. Then I can be Hop and get under those good tests and relax with Butter.

I remind myself of this again and again as Ms. Rubin walks around the room returning tests. Ms. Rubin always cups my test in her hand when she gives it back to me so that no one can see my shameful grade, and she puts it on my desk facedown so I can wait until I'm ready to look. To everyone else she returns tests face up, and she smiles. When Ms. Rubin returns a test to Katie, who sits next to me, Ms. Rubin touches Katie's shoulder because Katie is the smallest and cutest girl in my class.

My mother says that when I was little I was a wonderful student. She says that my kindergarten teacher told her I was the star of the class. Now my mother looks at me and says, *What happened? You used to love school.*

When Ms. Rubin puts my test face-down on my desk, I have to turn it over really slowly, starting with the bottom left-hand corner, so that I can see the red marks going from bottom to top, and when I'm sure all the X's I've seen mean that it's another F, I fold the test in half and in half again and then very calmly put it in my desk like it's really a fine grade and I'm just modest so I want to put it away and don't want to share my grade like everyone else is sharing their grades.

What I really want to do with my test is crumple it in my fist and punch myself with it. But I can't do that because I'm not allowed to punch myself at school. What I have to do instead is squeeze my empty fist into as tight a ball as possible and press my knuckles as hard as I can into the cold hard desk until I feel Butter coming toward me from my locker, just the feeling of Butter, but when I feel Butter coming toward me, I have to dig my knuckles even harder into the desk and grind them into the desk and then hold my right forearm with my left hand and dig my nails into my skin and then that's Butter digging her fingers into my arm because she's trying to lift my arm and make me punch myself. She says, "Why are you hitting yourself? Stop hitting yourself, you retard!" and she says it just like Helen says it when Helen is actually making me hit myself.

☙

If I wake up in the middle of the night and Hop and Butter have already been to Helen's room, I have to try to go back to sleep. Butter tries to hug me back to sleep, but if I'm still awake after fifteen minutes have passed, then she says, "You're Hop. Just be Hop," and that means I have to go down to the kitchen so that Butter can feed me. If I say I don't want to eat, Butter says, "You have to eat. You're getting too skinny, even for you."

The actual me is on a diet but not skinny at all. I only eat a snack once a week, on Wednesdays, when Helen is at Hebrew school, and I never eat the snacks that Helen likes best—the Doritos and Ring Dings—because those are Helen's special snacks and if I even taste them I feel terrible because Helen will want those snacks but they'll be gone because of me.

On Wednesdays I sit exactly where Helen usually sits on the couch and I put my feet where Helen puts her feet and I take big bites from my snack the way Helen does.

If you look at my mood chart, you can see that on Wednesdays my anxiety is a lot less, but Wednesdays are still my least favorite day of the week.

Hop never wants to eat anything at all, but when I can't sleep, Butter tells her she has to at least eat her Pop Tarts because that's her medicine, and the doctor says she has to eat two and if she can eat three, that's even better.

If I agree to eat two Pop Tarts, I get to sit under the kitchen table facing the wall, and Butter wraps one of her hands around each of my thighs to remind me that they are tiny Hop thighs and that's why I have to take my medication. If I start to think that I don't deserve the medication because my legs are too fat and nothing like Hop's or Helen's, Butter says, "The medicine will make you skinnier," and then she remembers I'm Hop and she says, "You need to eat." She tells me, "You're my special baby."

If I tell Butter that the Pop Tarts made me feel sicker, she says I just need more medicine and that I need liquid medicine and she walks me to the freezer and I have to eat the slightly melted rims around all the pints of ice cream we have because that ice cream melts into medicine. After I've eaten the melted rims I have to eat more ice cream if I still feel sick.

When I am standing in front of the freezer with the freezer door open, Butter stands behind me and puts her warm hands on my back and says, "Of course you're cold—look how skinny you are!" just like my mother says to Helen, and then Butter tries to be a blanket and wrap herself around me. Then I have to eat more ice cream and feel even colder until I really am cold skinny Hop.

Sometimes I hear my mother in my head asking who ate all the ice cream and then it is very hard to be Hop because there is no Hop and Helen is skinny and my mother is pregnant and they need our ice cream and I don't.

So Butter says, "You'll feel better if you eat some potato chips. Taking your liquid medicine always makes you nervous," and then I have to eat all of the broken potato chips in the bag and then just one whole chip and then I have to take more liquid medicine.

Butter says, "It'll soothe your stomach. I wish I could soothe you. I want you to feel as good as you possibly can." So I stand in front of the freezer and eat the ice cream with my fingers and then I feel better because I'm cold like Hop.

Then it's like a race to see how much ice cream I can eat before Hop turns into a boy and he gets so cold he dies. If that happens, I never get to be Hop again.

When I eat too much of the ice cream and I can't stop eating ice cream even though too much is missing and it's going to be obvious, Butter tries to hug me again, but I know what she's really doing is trying to comfort Hop, and I am not Hop. Then I hear my mom saying to my afternoon school teacher, *Maybe she should be nervous. I'd be nervous too if I were failing out of school.*

Even though I can feel Hop's medicine making me fatter, I keep eating the ice cream because it's already too late to stop. Hop is curled up by the vent at the bottom of the freezer where it's warmer, and then Butter has to get down on the ground too to protect Hop and then I know that what she's really doing is protecting Hop from me. I am pushing Butter farther and farther away from me and I am hurting Hop, and Butter has to love Hop instead of me, and even when I really am so cold I'm shivering, I don't deserve for Butter to warm me up because I made myself cold by eating Hop's medicine.

Then Butter yells, "Go!" And I have to run to the bathroom and push the handle of my special toothbrush as far down my throat as I can. My goal is to throw up so quickly that the ice cream is still cold when it comes back up. Then it feels like a cold cloud moving from low in my stomach up to my throat and collecting everything gross and hot inside of me and spitting it out again and again until I can feel a tiny bit of Hop at the core of me and I hear hard, steady thumping in my chest like an audience clapping for me to keep going faster and faster until there's no more cold cloud and what's left behind is warm special baby Hop expanding inside me, not like Hop is getting bigger but like Hop is blending and merging with the actual me until we're just Hop.

Then Butter knocks on the door and says, "Can I please come in now?" and she sits next to me even though what I want is for her to sit behind me and hug me. Instead she puts her hand on my stomach and says, "Poor thing, you're still sick." And then she says, "One more time," and I know if I do it two or three more times she'll press her chest to my back and hug me because I have actual tears in my eyes from throwing up so many times, and she says, "Okay, you're okay now," and it's like I've been crying and crying and finally I'm calm.

Then Butter says, "I'm worried about you, Gigi," just like Helen says to the actual Gigi, who is Helen's best friend, ever since Gigi told Helen what she really does with her toothbrush and why she giggles when she says to Helen, "Off to use my toothbrush!" after they've had a big snack.

I only use my special toothbrush in the middle of the night and on Wednesdays because I don't want Helen to know that I copied Gigi.

When I am finished and I've rehidden my special toothbrush under the sink, I get to curl up on the bathmat the way Hop curled up by the vent at the bottom of the freezer, and then Butter curls around me and we stay that way until we're falling asleep, and then we get to go back to bed and actually sleep.

⊗

The day before I have to take the first of my end-of-the-year tests, I have to hold the new baby for the first time. When they put my new sister on my lap, Helen stands over me and she keeps telling me to be careful and then I feel very nervous that I will drop the new baby or hit her because I don't like her, but then my dad tells Helen that I'm fine and that she should go talk to my mother, and my dad sits down not very close to me and looks at his phone and Butter comes and sits behind me and whispers, "It's okay; just do what I do," and she lightly rubs my arm and I do that to the baby.

The new baby's name is Hattie because my mother likes that name and Helen said she really wanted the baby to have an H name. I have a special feeling about the letter H because of the way it looks like two skinnies holding hands. Now it's like Hattie and Helen are those two H-skinnies, and I am the only one without an H name. My mother keeps calling the new baby *Sweetpea,* and Helen calls her *Baby H.*

I've been calling her Hattie, but when I am holding her and no one is looking, Butter says, "What if that's Hop?" Then she says, "She's beautiful. She looks just like you did when you were a baby," which is okay for her to say and for me to believe because my mother said the same exact thing. I am very thankful that Hattie is not skinny or blonde like Helen. It almost makes me want to cry I'm so relieved.

Butter puts her mouth right up to my ear and she whispers, "Hop, I love you so much."

Then I put my forehead to Hattie's forehead, so that our skin is touching but just barely, so that our eyes are looking right into each other. "You're Hop," I whisper, and I can feel her breathing onto my face. "Don't worry," I whisper. "You look like me, but you're Hop." Butter still has her mouth pressed to my ear, and her hand gets bigger on my arm and warmer. "I love you," I say to the baby Hop. "I will love you and protect you forever."

Then I put my fist to my mouth. I say to Butter, "I hate her. I can't." And when I move my fist to my ear, Butter says, "You can."

Acknowledgments

Thank you to the editors of the following journals who published earlier versions of my stories:

"The Logic of Imaginary Friends" in *Crazyhorse*
"The Twins" in *Black Warrior Review*
"This is Fatherhood" in *Kenyon Review*
"If I Could Have Anything, I'd Only Choose This" in *Masters Review*
"16 Days of Glory" in *New Ohio Review*
"Now We're Photogenic" in *The North American Review*
"Rough in Comparison" in *The Brooklyn Review*

Thank you to my sister, Sondra, my first reader, first confidant, and first friend—I love you always.

To my parents, Henrietta and Henry Rosenberg, who taught me to value art and education, whose hard work and generosity opened doors that have allowed me to spend my life learning and teaching, wondering, wandering, and making up stories.

To Maisie, for your love and protection, for taking me to storytime, and for all you taught me.

To Michael Greene, for letting us find you, for your interest and kindness, for your role in my drive to write, and for Sue.

To Paul Russell, whose novels showed me that every moment is full of potential and glory, whose attention made me feel like I have magic in me too. And to Vassar College—I wish I never had to leave.

To Kevin Canty, for challenging and encouraging me in equal measure, and for making me feel like I belonged in Montana, in some ways at least.

To Josh Tager, Michele Melnick, Leah Sugarman, Elizabeth Urschel, Steven Henry, Lauren Grasch, Adrienne West, David Galef, Felice and Craig Yeshion, Bob and Bobby Yeshion, Dottie and Les Roholt, and Carl Bradley—for your influence, for listening, for the feedback, inspiration, and encouragement.

To my nephew Nolan and my nieces Jordyn, Rachel, and Aly—I've loved watching you grow up. Some of what I've learned from it is hidden in these stories.

To Deborah Plachta, Wendy Miller, Benjamin Cheney, Christine Onorati, and Janine Ilsley, for their care, compassion, and wisdom.

To my sweet Greta, who makes every day so much better.

Finally, to Tiger, for insisting you'll love me forever, no matter how many times I say you can't know that—and for smiling when I say it, refuting my logic. What I know is that your hugs feel like sparkling magic tucked into a warm bed in a snowy cabin deep in the woods. I want them forever.

JILL ROSENBERG is a graduate of Vassar College and the MFA Program at the University of Montana. Her fiction has been published by the *Kenyon Review, Swamp Pink, Black Warrior Review,* and other journals. She currently writes and teaches in Montclair, New Jersey, where she also works with rescued cats and practices practicing Buddhism.

www.ingramcontent.com/pod-product-compliance
Ingram Content Group UK Ltd.
Pitfield, Milton Keynes, MK11 3LW, UK
UKHW040254160526
12510UKWH00002B/157